D0637333

"I don't inten... again."

Greer frowned. "Have you considered the possibility that you may fall in love again?"

"Love is the last thing I'm looking for. Once I have a nanny in place for Jamie, I'll be making another...arrangement."

"An arrangement?"

"A mistress," Colby replied. "What more could a single father want? A nanny to help look after his child...and a mistress to see to his other...needs."

Greer stared at him disbelievingly. "You can't be serious!"

"It'll be a business arrangement, Greer. I wonder...would you be interested in the job? You did say you aren't planning on marrying...."

Grace Green was born in Scotland and is a former teacher. In 1967 she and her marine-engineer husband, John, emigrated to Canada, where they raised their four children. Empty nesters now, they are happily settled in west Vancouver in a house overlooking the ocean. Grace enjoys walking the sea wall, gardening, getting together with other writers…and watching her characters come to life, because she knows that, once they do, they will take over and write her stories for her.

Grace Green has written for the Presents® series, but now concentrates on Harlequin Romance®…bringing you deeply emotional stories with vibrant characters.

Look out for *The Wedding Promise* (#3526) in October!

Books by Grace Green

HARLEQUIN PRESENTS
1323—TENDER BETRAYAL
1475—RISK OF THE HEART
1539—WINTER DESTINY

Don't miss any of our special offers. Write to us at the following address for information on our newest releases.

Harlequin Reader Service
U.S.: 3010 Walden Ave., P.O. Box 1325, Buffalo, NY 14269
Canadian: P.O. Box 609, Fort Erie, Ont. L2A 5X3

Colby's Wife
Grace Green

Harlequin Books

TORONTO • NEW YORK • LONDON
AMSTERDAM • PARIS • SYDNEY • HAMBURG
STOCKHOLM • ATHENS • TOKYO • MILAN
MADRID • WARSAW • BUDAPEST • AUCKLAND

If you purchased this book without a cover you should be aware that this book is stolen property. It was reported as "unsold and destroyed" to the publisher, and neither the author nor the publisher has received any payment for this "stripped book."

For my granddaughter, Kathleen

ISBN 0-373-17375-X

COLBY'S WIFE

First North American Publication 1998.

Copyright © 1997 by Grace Green.

All rights reserved. Except for use in any review, the reproduction or utilization of this work in whole or in part in any form by any electronic, mechanical or other means, now known or hereafter invented, including xerography, photocopying and recording, or in any information storage or retrieval system, is forbidden without the written permission of the publisher, Harlequin Enterprises Limited, 225 Duncan Mill Road, Don Mills, Ontario, Canada M3B 3K9.

All characters in this book have no existence outside the imagination of the author and have no relation whatsoever to anyone bearing the same name or names. They are not even distantly inspired by any individual known or unknown to the author, and all incidents are pure invention.

This edition published by arrangement with Harlequin Books S.A.

® and TM are trademarks of the publisher. Trademarks indicated with ® are registered in the United States Patent and Trademark Office, the Canadian Trade Marks Office and in other countries.

Printed in U.S.A.

CHAPTER ONE

'SELL it?' Greer whirled round from the corkboard where she'd just pinned a sketch of her latest lingerie design, an elegant satin-and-lace negligee in Midnight Cobalt. She stared at her grandmother with dismay. 'If I don't want the summer place on Lake Trillium you're going to *sell* it?'

'Correct.'

'But Gran...it's been in the family for generations!'

Leaning on her cane, Jemima Westbury moved across the office, skirting a table laden with bolts of purple, fuchsia and emerald silk, and stood with her back to the tall window overlooking Toronto's Spadina Avenue. The sun glistened in her silver topknot; its shadow softened the lines seventy-odd years had etched around her firm mouth and azure eyes.

'That's as may be,' she said, 'but *you* never go there anymore, and I?' She lifted one shoulder in an eloquent shrug. 'I no longer enjoy spending time there on my own.'

Greer frowned. 'I don't like the idea of strangers living at the cottage, Gran,' she said slowly. 'Oh, I know I haven't been to the lake for a couple of years but—'

Jem waggled the tip of her cane at her granddaughter. '*Eight* years. You haven't been there for *eight* years, not since that business with Bradley P—'

'Not since the summer Colby and Eleanor came home from Australia for his father's funeral.' Greer broke in hurriedly. 'I was seventeen.' She felt her cheeks flush. Stealing a moment to regain her composure, she crossed to her desk and flicked the switch that would silence the

5

music coming over the *Passing Fancy* workshop speakers. When she faced Jem again, her cheeks had cooled and she managed a rueful smile. 'You're right. It *has* been eight years.'

Briefly she wondered—as she had so often done—how much of the truth her grandmother had guessed that long-ago summer. Not all of it, Greer was sure—but certainly some. After all, wasn't Gran the one who had found her huddled down on the beach, dissolved in scalding tears, after Colby had flayed her with his scathing diatribe—

'What I'd like,' her grandmother was saying, 'is for the two of us to go up to the lake this week. You can make your decision there. If you don't want to keep the cottage, we'll start packing and get it ready for sale.'

'I really don't think I can get away.' Greer dropped her gaze; fidgeted with a scrap of Belgian lace on her desk. 'Since my *Vogue* cover, this place has been a madhouse—'

'Then I'll contact an agency and they can see to the arrangements. I think this is a good time of year to sell, don't you? Everything will be looking its best. Ben always said June was his favourite month at the lake—' Jem's voice caught, and shaking her head, she started for the door, her cane tapping unsteadily on the planked floor.

Greer had never met her grandfather—he had died before she was born—but she knew that after his death Jem had sold their large Toronto house and moved into an apartment. She had kept on the lakefront cottage because, as she had once confided to Greer, it was the only place where she could still sense Ben's presence and was thus very special to her.

Greer took in a deep breath, and ignoring the warning bells clanging in her head, hurried after the frail figure and caught her in the doorway. Clasping her grandmother's hands, she said quietly, 'I'll come, Jem darling, of course I'll come. But I can't get away till Friday. Friday afternoon...probably quite late.'

'Thank you, Greer.' Jem's voice trembled with pleasure. 'Thank you so much. Oh, we'll have a lovely trip, you'll see—just like old times.'

No, Greer reflected, stifling a bleak sigh as she escorted her grandmother to the elevator, it wouldn't be like old times. It could never be like old times again. Eleanor, and Brad Pierson, had seen to *that*.

She should have just told her grandmother the truth, she thought wearily—should have explained that though she had once loved going to the lake, it was a place she could no longer bear to visit. It was too filled with memories, memories of Colby, memories that tore her heart in two.

But she had committed herself to going.

And she could see no way out.

'When are we going to get there?' Jamie Daken's tone was sullen. 'How much farther do we have to go?'

'Another couple of miles, if I remember rightly.' Colby Daken glanced at the seven-year-old boy sitting slouched beside him. In the dim light from the Jeep's dashboard, he could see tousled black hair, shadow-smudged dark eyes, a drooping mouth. 'Tired?' he asked softly.

'Tired? Gosh, Dad, no—why should I be tired? The trip from Melbourne only took us from Wednesday till Friday, then we only took two hours to get through Toronto Customs, and we only got stuck in traffic for two hours getting out of the city. Now it's only—' he squinted through his glasses at the square watch strapped around his thin wrist '—five after midnight. Why should I be tired?'

The sarcasm in his son's tone set Colby's teeth on edge, but he decided this was neither the time nor the place to have a confrontation. Besides, Jamie was having a hard time dealing with his mother's death; Colby knew that only too well, and took the fact into consideration. This trip to Canada had been at the suggestion of their family doctor, after Colby had expressed his deep concern that although Eleanor had now been gone for six months, Jamie didn't seem to have made any steps toward accepting his loss.

'Your son, I believe, is feeling very much adrift,' Dr. Franks had said. 'He needs to have his roots re-affirmed—needs to get a sense of the *continuity* of things. Could you get away for a while—take him to Canada, show him where you grew up? Perhaps even spend some time at your cottage in Ontario—you did tell me you'd hung onto it, didn't you?'

Yes, he still owned the cottage, Colby had acknowl-edged. But he didn't explain to the doctor that the only reason he hadn't sold it when he'd flown to Ontario eight years ago for his father's funeral was that Eleanor had announced—while they were actually at the lake—that she was pregnant; and he—impractical in his delight— had decided to keep the place, in case the coming child might one day want it.

Who would have thought then, Colby reflected with a bitter twist of his lips, that Eleanor would die before her thirty-first birthday, and that he would one day be bringing that child here alone, in an attempt to bridge the wide gulf between them.

He felt something nudge his elbow, and looking down, saw that his son had fallen asleep and was lolling against him. Small, vulnerable . . . and defiant in his grief. Colby felt a powerful surge of love. Lifting a hand from the steering wheel, he carefully pulled the thin body into a more comfortable position.

As he glanced up again, the headlights danced among the trees ahead, illuminating three boards nailed to a post, at the entrance to a narrow track. On each weathered board was a name, burned into the wood:

Daken
Westbury
Pierson

Something sharp seemed to jab Colby's heart.

And as he swung the Jeep off the road, he frowned and moved restlessly in his seat. When he'd decided to make this trip, it had been for Jamie's sake; he hadn't given any thought to how he himself might be affected by this journey backward. Now he felt memories stumble from their hiding places, blink in the unaccustomed light and gradually evolve from their misty state into clearly visible form.

Memories of Greer.

Oh, God . . . he brushed a shaking hand over his eyes. Despite the years between, he could see her now as clearly as if she were walking along the track before him.

He'd always had a soft spot for the girl, but that last summer, the summer of her seventeenth birthday . . .

She'd been at Lake Trillium with her grandmother for a week before he and Eleanor had driven up there, and when he'd caught his first glimpse of her in three years, he'd felt a peculiar tightening in his throat. She had already acquired a lovely tan—the contrast between the nut brown of her skin and the stark white of her bikini had been breathtaking—but what had really struck him was the change in her hair. In the past, she'd always worn it in a ragged urchin style. Now it hung around her shoulders in a pale heavy sweep, the blunt-cut ends skimming like rich satin over high breasts that were already almost too lush for the sleek slenderness of her body.

She had, he realized, turned into a rare beauty.

But despite her new maturity, her green eyes had sparkled like sun-struck emeralds when she'd seen him, and with a delighted shriek she'd run up the beach and hugged him as enthusiastically as she'd always done as a child.

She was *truly* beautiful, and—he had thought—still as sweetly innocent as she had always been.

Which had made it all the more painful when he'd found her only three nights later with Brad Pierson— discovered her making love with the yuppie lawyer in a shadowed corner of the moonlit beach . . . actually heard her moan and cry out in ecstasy at passion's peak . . .

And all the while Brad's wife Lisa was in a Toronto hospital waiting to give birth to their third child.

Colby breathed out a harsh oath as the memory slashed through his heart.

Something had died in him that night. He'd never been able to tell what it was; he just knew it was some part of him that he would never find again. Oh, he'd been furious with Greer for her betrayal of Lisa—a true friend with whom they'd both had a warm and longtime relationship—and the following evening, when he'd at last caught Greer alone, he'd given vent to his rage and contempt with words he'd never used to a woman before.

He had also been unutterably disappointed in her; he had acknowledged that—though only to himself. But beyond that rage and contempt, and beyond that disappointment, there had been more. Something that had glittered at the edge of his consciousness, too far away, too nebulous, to grasp . . .

His headlights picked out the black and silver gleam of the lake ahead, and blowing out a self-derisive sigh, he gathered his thoughts back to the present. Lifting his foot from the accelerator, he let the Jeep coast down the slope toward the beach, braking gently as he rounded the corner, and guided the vehicle into the carport.

Only three cottages sat at this end of the lake, and his was closest to the track. Beyond it, behind a high cedar hedge, lay the Westbury cottage, and beyond that, separated from the Westbury's by birch trees and bushes, lay the Pierson's.

The place was deserted. No lights shone, no music played, no voices drifted through the fragrant night air...not like in the old days, when—

Memories. Oh, memories...

Jerking his thoughts away from the images beginning to press in again so mercilessly, he undid his seat belt, and Jamie's, and then he rounded the Jeep, opened the passenger door and scooped the sleeping child up in his arms.

'What...what...?' Jamie's voice was muffled against Colby's denim shirt. 'Mommy...?'

'It's all right, son.' Heart clenching, Colby tightened his arms around the slight body. 'We're here, at last.'

And as he dug into his hip pocket for the key to the cottage, he sent up an aching prayer that this little corner of paradise would achieve what he, on his own, had so far been unable to do.

Greer was glad she had come.

Relishing the feel of the dry white sand under her bare feet, she strolled along the deserted beach early Saturday morning. The day, she mused, was going to be a scorcher—the sky was forget-me-not blue and cloudless, the sun already drawing up a shimmering haze from the lake.

She felt relaxed ... far more relaxed than she had ever imagined she could feel here again, in this place ... and she knew why it was so.

It was because Colby Daken wasn't here.

Despite having assured herself last night on the drive north that he was in Australia and chances of bumping into him at the lake were nil, she had still felt as if she were balancing on a tightrope of tension that had become more and more nerve-racking with every mile that had gone by. On arrival at the foot of the track, she'd directed a swift apprehensive gaze in the direction of the Daken cottage, and her relief at finding the place boarded up had been so intense she'd become light-headed. As she and Jem had shared a pot of coffee outside after a late dinner, she'd been unable to keep that relief from showing.

'I've been foolish to stay away so long,' she'd admitted with a rueful smile. 'This—' she waved a hand around the veranda, its deck and white-painted Adirondack chairs washed pink by the final rays of the setting sun '—has got to be the most relaxing spot in the world.'

'You were afraid of facing up to the past' was Jem's blunt reply. 'But we all have our own garden of memories, darling, and just as in a garden—where we have to tear out invasive weeds so they won't choke the flowers we want to grow—in life we must haul all our darker memories out into the light...where they will, it is to be hoped, gradually die, allowing our sweeter memories room to flourish.'

Their eyes met, and there was so much compassion and understanding in her grandmother's that Greer felt a rush of love so profound it left her shaken. She pushed herself up from her low-slung chair and crossed to the railing, so her grandmother wouldn't see her tears. Hands cradling her mug, elbows on the rail, she blinked hard to clear her blurred vision as she looked out over the shadowy lake.

From the opposite shore could be heard the faint lilt of laughter, intermingling with the drifting strains of a tender love song; and in the gathering twilight, in air headily scented with the sweet fragrance from some unseen bush, fireflies flickered like tiny spurts of flame.

'So,' Jem's voice came to her quietly, 'do you think you'd like to keep the cottage after all?'

For a long moment, Greer didn't speak, and then, finally, she said in an equally quiet voice, 'Let me think it over, Gran.'

She turned and leaned back against the railing, meeting her grandmother's steady gaze in the dusk. 'I'll sleep on it,' she said, 'and I'll give you my answer tomorrow.'

And now tomorrow was here.

Greer walked a little way into the water. Sliding her hands into the pockets of her white shorts, she wandered along the fringe of the lake, lost in her thoughts.

Tomorrow was here...and yes, she had made up her mind.

Just after midnight, she had been wakened by some sound outside, and had found herself unable to get back to sleep. She had set herself to thinking about her grandmother's offer...her *ultimatum*...and in the end, after tossing and turning and agonizing for hours, she had made her decision.

Undeniably it did hurt to be here, but the alternative—to see the cottage fall into a stranger's hands—would hurt even more.

Besides, Jem was right—unhappy memories should be hauled out into the sunlight, and left in the scorching heat to wither and die—though she admitted she wasn't ready to face that task. Not yet. Perhaps later in the summer she would come back to the cottage on her own, with the sole purpose of confronting her memories and by doing so, finally heal the aching wounds in her soul...

And what a joy—and a triumph—that would be.

She stopped, with her back to the shore. Raising her face to the sky, her eyes closed against its brightness, she threaded her fingers through her hair and lifted it from her nape.

'Yes!' she said aloud, determinedly. 'Oh, yes!'

'Yes *what?*'

Greer spun round as the voice came from behind, a voice tinged with curiosity, but also edged with hostility and perhaps a trace of sullenness.

The child standing at the water's edge, feet planted challengingly apart, was a boy of about seven. He had an untidy sweep of black hair, and hazel eyes that glinted at her assessingly from behind a pair of dark-rimmed glasses. He was poking those glasses back up to the bridge of his nose, the movement automatic, as if habitual. His body was very thin and lightly tanned, and clothed only in a pair of multicolored baggy shorts that hung low on his hips.

'Yes what?' he repeated, scowling.

Greer waded out of the water, but when she reached the child, he stepped back, his gaze flicking over her hair, and over her face. Then, to her astonishment, she saw his eyes widen, his lips start to tremble. Good Lord, she thought, was she so terrifying a figure—or had the boy perhaps been *overly* cautioned to be wary of strangers?

'Hi,' she said, with what she hoped was a reassuring smile. 'Where did you come from? I thought I was alone.' She glanced along the beach toward the Trillium Lodge, a gracious mansion that sat atop a foundation of Precambrian rock about a mile and a half away. It had been built in the thirties by a wealthy New Yorker, as a summer home; now it was owned by a French couple, and run as an exclusive hotel. The boy, Greer decided, must be staying there.

'Why were you talking to yourself?' he demanded.

She shrugged. 'I'd been trying to make up my mind about something, and I'd finally decided my answer was going to be yes. Don't you ever talk to yourself?'

'Sometimes' was the grudging response.

Greer's tube top had slipped a little when she'd raised her hands to lift her hair; now as she felt the sun's heat begin to burn the tender skin on the upper swell of her breasts, she tugged the top back into place.

'I'm going in now, for a coffee,' she said, 'but first I'll walk you back along the beach. Your mother's probably worried about you.'

'I don't have a mother.'

Greer heard a quiver in his voice. 'Your dad then?'

'He's busy. He's making pancakes.'

He had an intriguing accent. English? South African? She found herself wondering why his father would be cooking breakfast if they were staying at the Lodge. 'You *are* at the Trillium Lodge, aren't you?' Frowning, she rested her hands lightly on her hips.

'No,' a cool male voice came from behind, 'he's at the cottage. With me.'

Australian. That was what the child's accent was. But now that she had finally fixed it, it was too late...

'Hello, Greer.'

Feeling as if her heart had stopped, Greer braced herself, braced every muscle in her body, and turned slowly.

'Colby.' It should have surprised her to see him, but somehow it didn't. That he was at the lake, after all, seemed now as inevitable to her as the rising and setting of the sun. 'What are *you* doing here?'

CHAPTER TWO

'SAME thing as you, I expect. Having a holiday.' Colby's eyes, black-fringed and even more strikingly blue than she remembered, locked with hers for a long moment, in a look so penetrating she had to brace herself not to flinch from it; and just when she was about to blink, his gaze fell to her mouth... making her wish, too late, that she had earlier applied a concealing coat of lipstick.

'Jamie—' he kept his gaze fixed steadily on her mouth as if he found it endlessly fascinating, and it was only with the greatest effort that Greer kept herself from running the tip of her tongue nervously over the vulnerable flesh '—your pancakes are ready. Maple syrup's on the table.'

'Okay.' Slouching, the child set off up the beach.

Colby frowned. He shifted his gaze, focused it on the small departing figure. *'Jamie?'* His tone was sharp.

The child hesitated, glanced back, muttered a strained 'Thanks' and then took off again, this time at a run.

'My son,' Colby said tersely. 'Jamie.'

His shirt was unbuttoned and as he slid a hand inside and rubbed his ribs in a frustrated gesture, Greer's gaze was drawn to the shadow of dark hair on his chest, hair that curled crisply and arrowed down beyond the low-slung waistband of his faded shorts. Dangerous, she decided with a tightening of her throat muscles, to venture further...

She forced her gaze up again, and drank in the absolute perfection of this man to whom she had long since gifted her heart. He seemed taller than before and leaner;

wider of shoulder and slightly more powerful of neck. His jaw was unshaven and his black hair carelessly swept back, the rakish effect making Greer's equilibrium wobble like Jell-O in an earthquake.

'Yes.' She kept her tone light, 'I gathered that.'

'How have you been?'

As he spoke, his bold gaze skimmed down over her figure, making Greer uncomfortably aware of how much flesh was revealed by her skimpy shorts and clinging tube top. 'I'm fine.' She tugged up the top though she had just minutes ago adjusted it and knew it was snugly in place. 'How about you, though? How are you coping? Jem and I...when we heard about Eleanor...it was such a shock—'

'Yes, it must have been a shock.'

'The funeral—we felt we should have been there, but—'

'The service was private—Eleanor wanted it that way. At any rate, she and your grandmother were never close—you were Jem's favorite, always—and as for *your* relationship with your cousin...' Colby's eyes held a cynical expression that was more eloquent than any words could have ever been.

Greer knew what he was thinking—he believed that she was the one responsible for the split between herself and Eleanor. If only he knew the truth. But he never would. Only three people had been aware of what had really happened that night in the shadowy corner of the moonlit beach—Eleanor, Brad...and herself. Eleanor was now gone, Brad would never tell...and she, Greer, had sworn to herself that she'd protect Colby from the truth forever because his happiness was the most important thing in the world to her.

'I didn't introduce you to Jamie because I have to talk with him first.' Colby's tone was cool. 'I had no idea you'd be here. When Jem wrote your aunt this spring, she mentioned to Cecilia that she was thinking of selling the cottage, so I expected it to be empty...or occupied by strangers. Eleanor never spoke of you to Jamie. I'll have to explain to him that you are related.'

'He seems...unhappy.'

'He's going through a rough time. That's why we're here.' Colby's lips twisted in a self-derisive smile. 'I used to be happy here—I thought perhaps he could be, too, in this Canadian Eden.'

Greer met his gaze. 'It *was* once an Eden,' she said, very quietly.

'But in every Eden there's a snake.'

He might as well have stabbed her in the heart.

At seventeen, wildly in love and irrational because of it, she'd felt a bitter resentment toward Colby for having judged and condemned her on evidence that though damning, was circumstantial; in view of their many summers together at the cottage she felt he should have *known* she wasn't that kind of girl. Men were so blind, she'd raged inwardly. So stupid. So easily fooled by the superficial.

Her cousin Eleanor with her baby-soft voice, her affected feminine fragility, her fake sugar-sweet smile, had fooled Colby into believing she was something she was not. He had fallen in love at first sight, bedazzled by the halo of outward beauty of a female who had in reality been—

Greer cut her thoughts off sharply. She should not be thinking ill of the dead. And of course she knew now that her resentment of Colby *had* been totally irrational. What *else* could he have thought, discovering her with Brad the way he had? She could even find it amusing, with a sort of black humor, that he had thought her capable of having a fling with a married man. After all, she'd been only seventeen at the time, and—sexually— as green as grass.

And wouldn't it surprise him to know, she reflected with a wryly self-deprecating smile, that even now, at the grand old age of twenty-five, she was still a virgin!

'You find that funny?' he rasped.

Greer blinked. 'Sorry...?'

'It amused you that—'

'Oh, the snake thing.' Greer twirled her index finger around a glossy strand of hair that had fallen over her bare shoulder. 'No,' she said lightly, 'I don't find that amusing. I was thinking of...something else.'

'Something else...or somebody else?' Colby's voice had a taunting edge. 'You're here with a man, of course.'

Deliberately, she threw him a flirtatious look from beneath her silky eyelashes. 'Hang around,' she said, her taunting tone an echo of his own, 'and you'll find out.'

Her left hand lay at her shoulder, the coil of hair loose around her fingers. Taking her by surprise, Colby reached out and, slipping her hand free, grasped it firmly. He inspected it, and raised one eyebrow.

'No ring?' His upper lip curled. 'He hasn't staked a claim yet?'

Greer snatched her hand back, dismayed by the current of electricity that had shot up her arm. 'A man can stake a claim without having to spend money on diamonds—'

'No ring, no claim,' Colby retorted. 'So...the field is wide open, mmm? Prize available to the highest bidder?'

Stunned at this side of Colby, a side she'd never known before, Greer was searching her mind for some snappy put-down when she heard her grandmother call to her.

'Greer, darling, coffee's ready. My goodness, is that Colby Daken? Hello there, you dear boy—what a delightful surprise! Come and join us, won't you?'

Colby grinned as he waved to Jem, who was standing on her veranda, her hair twisted up in a topknot, her spare figure adorned in an oversize shirt and drainpipe jeans. 'Hi, there, Mrs. W,' he called back. 'I'll take a rain check if I may—catch you later.'

His smile transformed his face, changed it to the face Greer knew of old—eyes twinkling, teeth sparkling white, deep grooves bracketing his beautifully sculpted mouth. She felt something melt inside her, and it had nothing to do with the growing heat of the morning sun.

But as her grandmother went inside again, his smile faded, and his lips were compressed tightly as he looked at Greer. 'You're here with your grandmother?'

'That's right. No man in tow.' Greer wrinkled her nose. 'Disappointed?'

'A little,' he returned, and went on smoothly, 'The chase is always more challenging when there's competition. A woman always seems more interesting when someone else wants her, too. And I'm sure you feel the same way about men. After all, wasn't that the appeal Brad Pierson held for you—he belonged to someone else?'

'I knew there was a reason I didn't want to come to the cottage this weekend.' Greer found her words coming out with exactly the right edge of weary boredom she wanted to express. 'There was always the chance you might be here.'

He ignored her jibe. 'You're here only for the weekend? You're going back to town tomorrow?'

'That's right,' Greer said coolly. 'I'm here only because Jem asked me to come with her.'

'*Is* she going to sell the cottage?'

'That's going to be up to me.'

Colby raised his eyebrows.

'My grandmother doesn't like spending time here on her own any more,' Greer explained stiffly. 'At least, that's what she told me. I think there's more to it.'

'Such as?'

Greer shrugged. 'Gran sold her Buick in February, around the time her driving licence was due for renewal, and I suspect the Motor Vehicles Branch may have called her in for a test that she failed...her eyesight's not as good as it once was...and she's too proud to admit it. At any rate, she no longer has transportation to get here, so she's told me the property is mine, if I want it. And if I don't—'

'Then she's going to unload it.' Colby's eyes narrowed as he looked at Greer. 'So...what are you going to do?'

I thought I knew...but now that you're here, Lord knows what my decision's going to be! 'I haven't made up my mind yet. I told Jem I'd let her know today. If I don't take her up on her offer, we'll get the place ready for sale. Now—' Greer turned to walk away '—if you'll excuse me—'

'Wait.' He caught her arm.

'What?' She was so close she could smell the musk of his hair, the dizzying scent of his skin...so close that if she wanted to, she could have run her fingertips over the hard sculpted angle of his jaw. And she wanted to. Oh, how she wanted to.

'I'll bring Jamie over, after breakfast, to meet his great-grandmother. And because you're here, I'll have to introduce him to you, too—'

'Well, sorry about that,' Greer snapped, snatching her arm free, 'but yes, I think that would be a good idea. He was taken aback when he saw me...I realize now it was probably because of the family resemblance. I must remind him of...his mother.'

Their eyes locked, and in Colby's she saw something she hadn't noticed before. A look of deep and private pain.

Greer felt a sudden stab of remorse, remorse that twisted her heart, and she had to ram her hands deep into her pockets to keep from reaching out to comfort him. Oh, how she ached for a return of the days when she could have done just that...

But those days were gone. Long gone.

And they would never return.

'Colby, I'm sorry,' she said, huskily. 'It must still hurt, I know, to talk about Eleanor. You must miss her so.'

Fighting back a welling of tears, she turned away quickly so he wouldn't see her distress, and set off up the beach toward the cottage.

This time, he didn't try to stop her.

'So... Colby is here.'

'Yes.' Greer tried to keep a lid on her roiling emotions as she met her grandmother's shrewd azure gaze unflinchingly across the pine kitchen table. 'He's here.'

'Alone?'

'Jamie is with him.'

'Mmm. And missing his mother dreadfully, I should imagine.'

'Seems that way.' Greer moved restlessly on her chair. 'His father said he's been having a rough time. He hopes, I think, that a summer at the lake will help Jamie come to terms with his loss.'

'And Colby? How does he seem?'

'Hard.'

Her grandmother raised her eyebrows.

Greer frowned, feeling unaccountably irritable and impatient. 'He's—'

She broke off, searching for a word that would describe Colby's attitude toward her, without giving too much away, but before she could find one, Jem said, in a questioning tone, 'Grieving?'

'When he came back here after his father died, he was grieving.' Greer fidgeted with the beaded edge of her place mat. 'But he was still... nice.' Oh, Lord, had he ever been nice! He had... during those first three days at the lake, before the Bradley Pierson affair... treated her like a cherished and dearly missed friend.

'Colby sounded pleasant enough when he spoke to me.'

'Oh, yes, the man can be pleasant when—'

'Colby.'

Greer blinked. 'Sorry?'

'Colby.' Jem lifted the coffeepot from its spot on the table and refilled her mug. She added a spoonful of sugar, and stirred it in, before saying, in a gentle voice, 'His name is Colby, dear. It won't hurt you to say it.'

'I don't want to say it!' The outburst was childish, and Greer was ashamed of it... and of herself. She was twenty-five, no longer a child of seventeen, hurting and lonely. She pushed back her chair and got to her feet. 'Jem, about the cottage. I thought this morning that I'd really like for us to keep it in the family... but now that...he...is here, I'm going to need some more time.'

'Time for what?'

'Time to find out what his plans are. If he intends to be here every summer, it would be an impossible situation. I could never relax, with him around... treating me like some sort of a... leper.' Her voice cracked, and she crossed to the window. Gripping the edge of the countertop, she looked out...

A mistake. Straight ahead, slung between two ancient birch trees, was the hammock where she and Colby had cavorted together many times in happy summers gone by. Oh, Lord...

'You love it here, just as much as I do,' Jem said. 'Greer, I've been thinking. The cottage, as you reminded me when we talked in your office, has been in the family for generations. Five generations, to be exact. Let us not make any hasty decisions. Now that I'm here, I'd like to stay, for the rest of the summer—'

Greer whirled around, aghast. 'Gran, I can't *possibly* stay with you! I've told you how busy I am—'

'Darling,' Jem soothed, 'I'm not suggesting that. What I *am* suggesting is that you join me on the weekends. You say Colby and my great-grandson are going to be here all summer—what a splendid opportunity it will be

for me to get to know the child! And it will be good for
him to get to know me.'

Her eyes had a spark of excitement that Greer hadn't
seen there in a while, and as she saw it, guilt stung her
conscience. Oh, she didn't neglect her grandmother—in
fact, she made a point of seeing her several times a week,
and she took her to the theater on a regular basis—but
she had to admit her work took precedence. She'd buried
herself in it for years, in an attempt to shut out her
painful memories; and now she realized with a shock
that she hadn't given as much of herself as she perhaps
should, to this wonderful, generous woman who had
done so much for her.

She crossed to her now, and bending down, gave her
a tight hug. 'You're right, Gran—it's not the kind of
thing that should be decided overnight. And especially
it's not the kind of thing that should be decided on the
basis of who our next-door neighbors might be! If you're
sure you won't mind being on your own through the
week, that's fine with me. I can't promise, though, that
I'll be able to make it every single weekend, but I'll try.'
She straightened, and managed a bright smile. 'There,
how does that sound?'

'Sounds wonderful—'

A loud *rat-tat* rattled on the screen door, and when
Greer looked around and saw Colby on the veranda, she
felt a surge of dismay. How long had he been standing
there? How much had he overheard? But before she
could recall exactly what she'd been saying, Jem had
scooped up her cane and moved across the room, clicking
up the latch and opening the door.

'Well, Colby,' she began, pleasure warming her voice,
but before she could go any further, Colby had swung
her up in his arms and enfolded her in a bear hug.

'You're a sight for sore eyes, Jem Westbury.' His voice
was gruff. He dropped her gently to the floor, but took
her hands in his and looked down into eyes that were

hazed with tears. 'Lord, it's good to see you. Jamie—'
he put an arm around the shoulders of the boy trying
to hide behind him, and pulled him forward '—I'd like
you to meet your great-grandmother, Jem Westbury.
Jem, my son, Jamie.'

Jem looked long and searchingly at the boy. In the
end, she nodded, her expression satisfied. 'You're a
Daken,' she said bluntly, 'and that's good.' And as Jamie
pressed back against his father, she added, chucklingly,
'Oh, you needn't worry that I'm going to hug you and
kiss you the way your father has just done with me. Mind
you, I liked it, but that's because I'm a woman, and we
love to be fussed over. Maybe one day, though, when
we get to know each other better, you'll feel like giving
me a hug. I'll welcome it when you do. Now what do
you want to call me, young man? Great-grandmother's
a bit of a mouthful, don't you think?'

'Your name's Mrs. Westbury,' Jamie said in a flat
voice. 'That's what I'll call you.'

If she was taken aback, Jem showed no sign of it.
'That'll be just fine,' she said. 'Now, you've already met
my granddaughter, Greer...Greer Alexander, who
is—'

'Dad told me. She's my mother's cousin.'

And Greer guessed, from the indifference in his voice,
that he was going to announce that he would call her
Miss Alexander. Quickly she said, 'That's right, Jamie.
Your great-grandmother Jem had two children, Lorna
and Taylor. Lorna got married and had one child...that
was me, and Taylor got married and had one child...that
was your mother. And since I don't have any nephews
or nieces, nor shall I ever, I'd be really happy if you'd
call me Aunt Greer.'

She knew she had put him on the spot. How could
he refuse...without seeming churlish?

He scowled, and she sensed he had guessed her
strategy. She could almost hear him say to himself: The

battle is on and she's won the first round! Jem had drawn
Colby over to the table and they were chatting as Jem
poured him a mug of coffee, but her own attention was
fixed on Jamie as he searched for a response that would
make him the winner of the next round. Her mouth
threatened to curve in amusement; she primmed it and
waited.

'I thought you looked like Mommy when I saw you
on the beach.' Jamie's hazel eyes glinted smugly. 'But
you don't.' He tilted his small chin and went on in a
voice that was meant for her ears only, 'You're not nearly
as pretty.'

Momentarily shocked, Greer wrapped her arms around
herself. A defensive gesture, she knew. Yet why should
she feel she would have to defend herself against this
child? He was, after all, only seven. 'You're right,' she
said evenly, 'I'm not nearly as pretty as your mother
was.'

'And my dad loved her more than anybody in the
world.'

'Yes, he did.' Greer fought an urge to take the little
boy into her arms and soothe away the hurt and anger
she could feel emanating from him. Did Colby realize
how *deeply* affected his son was by the loss of his
mother? She hoped so, and she hoped he had the tools
to deal with the problem. A summer at the cottage was
wonderful for any child...but for this particular child
she sensed that more, much more, was needed.
'Jamie—' she looped a strand of her hair back over one
ear '—I think I may have an old photo album with pictures of your mother. Would you like me to fetch it?'

'Now?' His glasses slipped down; he flicked them back
up onto the bridge of his small nose.

'Sure...if you like.'

'Darling.' Jem touched Greer's arm. 'Pour yourself
another mug of coffee and let's all go out onto the
veranda. It's far too nice a morning to waste indoors.

Here.' She handed Jamie a frosted tumbler, and as Colby held the door open, she put a hand on Jamie's shoulder and guided him outside. 'Try this—lemonade, my own special recipe.'

Colby waited for Greer to follow, but she shook her head. 'Go ahead,' she said stiffly. 'I promised Jamie I'd show him some pictures of Eleanor.' She hesitated, and then went on in a voice that couldn't be heard outside, 'I think it will be good for him—being here, I mean, and getting to know Jem. She has a wonderful way with children.'

She thought she saw Colby's face soften. 'She was here for me when my own mother died,' he said. 'I was only four, of course, when Dad bought the cottage, but from that very first summer, she was a part of my life. Dad often said how much we both owed her—'

'She got as much as she gave, Colby—perhaps even more. It's so often the case, when we reach out to help someone.'

Colby leaned against the wall with one shoulder, and folded his arms. 'Tell me something,' he said softly.

Greer felt her heartbeats stumble. 'If I can.'

'Why are you so sure you'll never have any nieces or nephews?'

'Oh, that.' Greer looked away from him, fixing her gaze on the pine dresser crammed with Jem's antique dishes. She shrugged. 'I don't have any brothers or sisters, so—'

'You know what I mean.' Colby's voice demanded she look at him; she didn't. She let her gaze drift to the copper pots and pans dangling from a wooden beam on the ceiling above the sink. 'When you marry there's every likelihood in the world that you'll end up with a horde of nephews and nieces ... and if you keep the cottage, you can invite them all here for the summer, to play with your own children.'

Children. The only children she had ever dreamed of having were Colby's. And that was never to be. The ache in her heart was an old ache, but age made it no easier to bear. 'I don't plan on getting married,' she said, forcing herself at last to meet his gaze... and seeing him frown. 'Now, if you'll excuse me, I want to go and get that old album for Jamie.' Turning, she quickly left the kitchen, and was thankful to hear no sound of footsteps following her as she hurried along the lobby.

What would he think, she wondered dismally, if he knew that *he* was the reason she'd never marry, because she had never met anyone who could hold a candle to him? Oh, at first she *had* made a valiant effort to erase her memories of him and fall in love with someone else... but all she had to show for it were two failed relationships—relationships that had both foundered when the men involved had finally pressed for commitment and intimacy, neither of which she had been able to give, because her heart belonged to Colby.

She blinked back a tear as she crossed the sitting room. How would he feel if he knew she loved him... and loved him in the same single-minded way he'd loved Eleanor?

It was ironic that if she herself hadn't been so besotted with Colby that she took snaps of him at every opportunity, Eleanor would never even have contrived to meet him, and there would have still been a chance, if only ever-so-faint a chance, that Colby would have waited for her to grow up...

Greer sank onto the hooked rug by the pine corner cabinet, and pulling open the door of the lower cupboard, hauled out a pile of albums. As she reached for the green one, containing photos of Eleanor and Colby, another album tumbled out... a heavy leather-bound brown one...

With a defeated sigh, she took the album in her lap, and let it fall open.

Her eyes blurred as she stared at the five-by-seven enlargement of Colby. No coincidence that the page had opened at this place...it had always been her favorite photo, and she had spent countless hours gazing at it. She found herself smiling now, wistfully, as she recalled the occasion on which she'd taken the original snap....

Jem had made three blueberry pies that breezy August morning, and had arranged two on the sill of the kitchen's passing window to cool. She'd given Greer the third to take over to Lisa...and when Greer was on her way back, she'd noticed Colby sneaking across the veranda, his purpose blatantly obvious. She'd whipped inside for her camera, and had returned in time to catch Colby with his thumb in a pie.

But a second before she pressed the shutter, he must have sensed her presence. He looked around abruptly, and on seeing Greer, had let out a great guffaw of laughter; she had snapped the picture, and when it was processed a week later, she had felt her insides turn to mush. Colby's eyes sparkled with laughter and delight, his features were creased in a devastatingly attractive 'Oh, Lord, caught in the act!' grin, and his hair had fallen over his brow giving him a devil-may-care look that would have melted the coldest heart.

And her heart hadn't been cold.

It had been burning hot, with a passion that at the tender age of fourteen had mystified—and frightened—her.

She'd taken the album with her to Australia, when she'd gone there as usual to spend the last fortnight of the summer holidays with her aunt Cecilia, before returning to Toronto and school in the Fall.

Eleanor had, of course, been at home—she invariably chose to spend all her summers with her mother, loving the laid-back life-style...the live-in maid, the endless parties, the attention lavished on her by her mother's women friends.

And Eleanor had come on Greer one morning as Greer lay on her bed staring at the treasured photo of Colby.

'What's this?' her nineteen-year-old cousin had asked lazily. 'A picture of some movie star? Don't tell me you're one of those mindless teenagers who send adoring fan letters to their current heartthrobs.'

Greer hadn't answered. Let Eleanor think that if she wanted; she had no desire to share her secret with anyone. But her silence had made Eleanor curious. Her cousin had snatched up the album ... and had then of course noticed the black writing scrawled over the foot of the photo:

> *To my summer sprite*
> *Love from Colby*

For a few moments the silence in the room had hummed as Eleanor had assimilated this information. Then ...

'Colby Daken.' Eleanor's tone was cool. 'Gran's mentioned him once or twice. He's the one whose father owns the summer cottage next to hers?'

'That's right.'

'Are they ... well-off?'

Greer shrugged. 'I think so. Actually yes—Colby's father, Mackenzie Daken, owns Daken Construction—one of the biggest construction companies in Canada. The family has pots of money. But you'd never know it,' she hastened to add, 'they're just ... well, ordinary, I guess. Really nice.'

The following summer, for the first time, Eleanor had invited herself to the cottage at Lake Trillium for the whole of July and August. Greer had been astonished, and Jem had been, too. Eleanor had never hidden her disdain for cottage life—for 'roughing it,' as she scornfully put it—and it wasn't till Greer saw her beautiful cousin setting her cap for Colby, that she finally realized what was going on. But she'd never told anyone ... not even her grandmother...about Eleanor seeing the picture of Colby and asking if the family had money—

'Have you found it?'

Jamie's voice coming from right behind her made Greer start. Snapping the album shut, she stuffed it back into the cupboard, and then tugged the green album from the pile.

'Here—' she brushed off a trace of dust with her fingertips '—it's yours, if you want to keep it.'

Jamie took the album but didn't open it. Clutching it against his chest, he took in a deep breath, opened his mouth as if he wanted to say something, then closed it again. His gaze drifted over her hair, and her face. He raised his hand, and Greer thought he was going to flick up his glasses. To her astonishment, what he did was reach out and touch the top of her head, letting his fingers slip over her hair, as if he wanted to experience the texture of it.

Emotion tightened Greer's throat muscles. Was Jamie remembering how his mother's hair felt? Eleanor's hair had been ash blond, too, though not quite as thick, nor as silky as hers. 'Jamie,' she whispered, huskily—and lifted her hand to touch his...but he snatched it away. Wrapping both arms around the album, he took off like a frightened rabbit.

She thought she heard a sound like a gulping sob as he reached the door, but when she went out onto the veranda a minute or two later, she found him sitting on the swing, drinking his lemonade.

And when their eyes met, he looked at her as coolly as if the episode in the sitting room had never taken place.

CHAPTER THREE

'GREER has done very well for herself,' Jem said as Greer moved across the veranda. 'The *Passing Fancy* label has really taken off. Tell Colby, dear, about your new workshop on Spadina Avenue!'

'A workshop on Spadina?' Colby had gotten to his feet when Greer came outside; now, as she perched her hip on the railing, he dropped back into his chair. 'So,' his tone was light, 'you made your dream come true after all.'

'It was a goal,' Greer said quietly, her gaze dropping to the mug of coffee nestled in her hands. 'Not a dream.' The achievement of a goal needed only drive, talent, hard work . . . and luck. Dreams were different. Dreams required magic to make them come true. Goals and dreams. She had had one compelling goal, and one shining dream.

She and Colby had sat on this veranda more times than she could remember, her eyes sparkling with excitement, his with determination, as they talked about their goals. Hers: to become a respected and successful lingerie designer with a workshop on Toronto's Spadina Avenue. His: to work with his father, learn everything he could about the business, and eventually have his own branch of Daken Construction. Of her secret shining dream she had never spoken—Colby was the last person to whom she could have spilled out this most cherished part of her soul, because he, Colby, was at the very heart of it. And he had never spoken to her of any dreams—at least, not till after he'd fallen in love with Eleanor; then he could talk of nothing else—

'A goal, then.' Colby sprawled back lazily. 'And, if my memories serve me correctly, you've achieved it a couple of years earlier than you'd expected to.'

'Greer?' Jem's tone was curious.

'Yes, Gran—I'd always planned on having my own place, even when I was a little girl playing with cutout dolls and paper dresses...but he's right. I hadn't expected to get there quite so soon.'

'Nothing to be proud of in your case, young lady,' Jem said bluntly. 'If your life had been balanced, if you'd been involved in a steady relationship with a man—and if that man had been worth his salt—you'd have had to spend less time working, and more time just plain living.'

'I've had men in my life,' Greer protested stiffly, her cheeks hot with mortification as she sensed Colby's gaze on her. 'You know I have. Nick Westmore, and Jared Black—you met them both, you *liked* them both! At least you said you did—now you claim not even to *remember* them!'

'Oh, way back *then!*' Jem's expression was scornful. 'Now it's a different man every Friday night! Easy come, easy go! What ever happened to commitment—isn't that the modern buzzword for what my generation called love?'

Greer treated her grandmother to a glare that would have withered any normal person but only seemed to intensify the challenging glitter in Jem Westbury's eyes.

'If you'll excuse me.' With a haughty tilt of her chin, Greer slid off the railing. 'I think I'll go for a walk.'

Colby got to his feet, and Jem pushed herself up, too. Leaning on her cane, she addressed Jamie.

'Young fella,' she said briskly, 'I brought some tomato plants from the city and they have to be put in the ground. I need someone to help me, someone handy with a watering can. I don't suppose you'd like the job? Of course, you'd have to take off your sneakers, and puddle about in the earth and probably get awfully wet and mucky—'

'I'm not allowed to get dirty. Mommy doesn't like—' Jamie broke off abruptly, his cheeks suddenly bright pink.

Jem blinked in surprise, and Colby stood gazing at his son as if the boy was a complete mystery to him. Greer realized she was the one who was going to have to respond to the child's comment.

'Jamie?'

He looked at her with obvious reluctance, and she gave him another of her reassuring smiles. 'Honey, things are different here at the lake. Nobody minds when we get grubby, it's just part of cottage living, and it's one of the very nicest parts. I'm sure your mommy didn't want you getting dirty when you were in your school clothes, or when she took you for outings, or when she had friends in, but—'

'I wasn't to get dirty. Ever.' Jamie's eyes glistened, but small muscles flexed determinedly in his jaw. 'I *won't* get dirty. You can't make me.'

Good grief, thought Greer, what kind of upbringing had Eleanor subjected her son to? Telling a boy he mustn't ever get dirty?

'Then you must come and watch me,' Jem said firmly. 'I'm going to get *very* dirty, and when I'm done, if you like you may turn the hose on my bare feet and legs and wash them off. Does *that* appeal?'

Jamie's glasses slid down his nose. He pushed them up, and to her surprise, Greer saw the beginnings of a wavery smile tug the corners of his mouth.

'All right,' he said gruffly. 'I can do that.'

'Good lad.' Jem held the screen door open for him, and they went inside, the door swinging shut behind them. As the snap of the catch echoed, and then faded, Greer became all too aware that she and Colby were now alone.

'Well,' she said tersely, stepping quickly away from him, across the deck, 'I'm off then.'

He caught up with her as she reached the short flight of steps leading from the veranda to the beach area. 'Not so fast.' He grasped her forearm. 'Where are you going?'

The touch of his fingers on her bare skin sent a tingle of sensation rippling through her, a sensation that was as pleasurable as it was disturbing. She shook herself free. 'Don't you listen?' She looked up at him... and wished she hadn't. The blue of his eyes bedazzled her; the arrogant tilt of his head alarmed her. 'I'm going for a walk.'

'I'll join you.'

'I don't want you to join me. I want to be left alone.' Her voice had a breathless quality. 'I have some thinking to do—'

'About the cottage?'

'Yes.' How unfair that a man should have such lustrous and seductively long black eyelashes. 'About the cottage.'

'We can stand here all day,' he said equably, 'with you refusing to walk unless I go away... which I warn you I'm not about to do... or we can stroll along the beach... together. I'm going to be here for the summer, your grandmother tells me you'll be spending most of your weekends here, too. You apparently don't have a man in your life at the moment, and at present I am also unattached. We have a history, you and I... so why don't we add to it!' His lips twisted in a smile. 'Just a summer affair, Greer—what do you think?'

Had Greer not been so stunned by his suggestion, she would have cut him off the moment he made it. But she *was* stunned... and not only stunned, outraged. Yet to be honest she had to admit he must feel it perfectly in order to make such a suggestion; after all, when she was seventeen she had allowed him to believe she'd slept with Brad Pierson... and just minutes ago her grandmother had remarked on her 'easy come, easy go' relationships with men. What Gran didn't know was that the men she dated now were—because she wanted it that way—just friends, and nothing more.

'You're suggesting we have an affair?' Greer raised her eyebrows mockingly. 'In spite of my... promiscuous behavior? Don't you think that might be dangerous— for you—all things considered?'

'There are ways to... get around... that.' A breeze gusted from the lake, tossing a heavy strand of hair over his forehead; gold gleamed at his wrist as he raised a hand and impatiently raked the strand back into place.

'You've changed a lot.' He really had beautiful hands, she reflected distractedly; long-fingered, elegant, with neatly trimmed spatulate nails. Just watching him thread those fingers through his glossy black hair had sent an odd dark shiver spiraling to some indefinable place deep inside her. 'You're not the man I once knew.' Her tone was icy. 'You say we have a history. We do, and that's all it is. History! As far as I'm concerned *you* are history!'

He sidestepped her and blocked her way as she tried to go down the stairs. Now that he was standing on the step below her, their faces were on the same level... and she was staring right into those lethal blue eyes.

'I've always found it impossible to understand,' he said roughly, 'why someone as lovely as you would need to look to a married man like Brad Pierson for satisfaction. You could have had any man you wanted. Why did you have to set out to seduce him? Good God.' His voice had hardened. 'I'd known him for years and I'd have sworn he was the last person to have gotten involved in an adulterous affair.'

'You thought you knew Brad but you didn't. You thought you knew me but you didn't.' Greer couldn't keep the bitterness from her tone as memories of that long-ago summer rushed in again...

And shock froze her as, with a swift and totally un-expected movement, Colby grasped her by the shoulders and jerked her toward him. Before she could even gasp, he took her mouth in a deliberate and soul-shattering kiss.

It was over in a few seconds. Nothing was left of the abrupt assault but his harsh breathing, and her own...and the bruised tingling of her lips. She and Colby had never touched before, in any sexual way. This...this attack had her cringing from him as surely as if he slapped her.

'Don't ever,' she whispered raggedly, 'try to do that again.' She stared at him through blurred eyes, seeing the dark mass of his hair, the bronzed color of his face, the brilliant blue of his eyes...

The cynically twisted slash that was his mouth.

He had kissed her. In days gone by she would have sold her soul for one kiss, just one kiss, from Colby Daken.

She would never have believed it would come to this. A tiny sob escaped her, before she could stifle it.

'Very good,' he said softly. 'Very convincing. And oh, my God, very tantalizing. This summer—' slowly, eyes never leaving hers, he ran the tip of his index finger over the chiseled curve of his upper lip, as if he would capture and store forever the memory of his stolen kiss '—is going to be far more fun than I'd expected. And before it ends, my darling Greer, I shall take you to my bed. And there I'll find out just what it is about you that can make a man like Bradley Pierson succumb to your advances while his wife is in hospital waiting to give birth to their child. A challenge.' His breath hissed in through narrowed nostrils. 'That's what you are. And one I accept.'

With a self-assured swing of his shoulders, he turned away and bounded down the steps. A moment later, she heard him open the screen door at the east side of his cottage; and then she heard the door clatter shut again.

Her mind in turmoil, Greer walked slowly down the steps, across the lawn and out onto the sandy white beach.

Why had she agreed to come with Gran to the cottage? Oh, what a mistake that had been. How she wished she had never come...

Still, when she thought of Jamie, and his troubled little mind, she acknowledged that perhaps something good would come out of this summer. Jem would get to know her great-grandson, and with her wonderful way of dealing with children, she might well be the means of drawing the boy from his state of unhappiness and confusion.

Had it not been for that, she would have reneged on her promise to Jem, and insisted they go back to the city right now.

She couldn't. There was Jamie to consider.

She would just have to handle Colby as best she could, when he started his campaign to get her into his bed.

For that must never happen.

If she slept with him, he would discover she was a virgin. He would know she had never slept with Brad Pierson....

And he would have no option but to come up with another scenario, one that had obviously never crossed his mind.

It was Eleanor who had been involved with Brad. Eleanor, Colby's own wife, the woman he'd loved so blindly it had verged on idolatry... and it would have destroyed him, Greer had believed then and still believed now... if he'd discovered she had betrayed him.

And this, of course, was why she'd agreed to cover up for her cousin. Oh, not for Eleanor's sake—she had despised the woman for her adulterous behavior—but for Colby's, to protect him from the truth that would have shattered him.

Now all Colby had left of his wife were his precious memories. And she, Greer, would do anything in her power to keep those memories intact.

Lisa Pierson and her three children turned up at Lake Trillium that afternoon.

Greer didn't see them arrive. She'd gone out to the shed in the backyard after lunch, and had spent a couple of hours sorting out tools and planters and half-empty packages of this, that and the other, telling herself she was just getting things organized in case Jem had to sell the cottage . . . but all the time knowing in her heart that she was trying to avoid Colby.

Around four-thirty, she had just flopped down on an old tree stump outside the shed, and was wiping a grubby hand over her brow, when she heard the back door of the cottage swing open. Expecting to see Jem, she looked up with a smile . . . the smile changing to an exclamation of astonishment when she saw the woman coming down the path toward her, a petite brunette in her late thirties, dressed in a navy blouse and a pair of shorts.

Greer stumbled to her feet. 'Mrs. *Pierson?*'

Lisa Pierson's eyes glowed with pleasure. 'Greer, I couldn't believe it when Jem said you were here. I thought you'd given up on cottage living!'

Greer made a helpless gesture with one hand. 'Is it really you? You look great—so slim and—'

She broke off, grimacing. But even as she started to murmur an embarrassed apology, Lisa laughed delightedly.

'Don't apologise, honey—it took two long years to lose those extra fifty pounds, and believe me, there's nothing I like more than people complimenting me on my changed appearance. But you—' she embraced Greer,

and then stood back to examine her '—you look pretty
wonderful yourself.'

Greer chuckled. 'I hardly think so, Mrs. Pierson—I
must look a sight, all cobwebs, and dust, and—'

'Oh, drop the Mrs. Pierson, please!' Lisa rolled her
eyes. 'You're no longer a little girl . . . besides, you make
me feel ancient. Call me Lisa. Look, I've got to dash—
the kids and I just got here and I've left them unloading
the van—but I'll see you later. Jem has told me just
enough about your successful career to whet my appetite—if I have one weakness, it's gorgeous silk lingerie!
But we'll have loads of time to talk about that. I've
brought enough steaks to feed an army and you and Jem
are coming over for a barbecue. Around seven. Give us
time to settle in. Okay?'

Greer knew, from Jem's reports over the past several
summers, that Lisa and her husband were still married,
and still, apparently, happy together, but it sounded as
if, on this trip at least, Lisa and the children were here
on their own. Perhaps Brad was too busy at work to get
away. Greer hoped that was the case; it was enough that
she'd had to face Colby, without having to be in the
company of the man she was supposed to have seduced
into an illicit affair.

But even if Brad had been there, how could she have
gotten out of the invitation? What possible excuse could
she have come up with that would hold water? Besides,
as far as she was aware, Lisa knew nothing of the incident that long-ago summer; she, Greer, would make
sure it remained a secret. 'I'll look forward to it,' she
said. 'Thanks a lot.'

'Great. See you around seven.'

Greer stood watching Lisa bounce away along the
path, her short brown hair as sleek as a seal's, her trim
behind attractively set off by her striped shorts and the
shapely curve of her legs enhanced by the heels of her
espadrilles.

Brad Pierson, Greer reflected wearily, was one very lucky man. Why would he ever have been foolish enough to risk losing a wife like Lisa?

She went back into the shed, but somehow, she had lost the zest for cleaning. It was too hot, of course...but Lisa's visit had opened the doors to the past and, despite Greer's earlier decision not to haul out her unhappy memories till later in the summer because she still felt too vulnerable to confront them, those memories—driven by forces over which she had no control—came rushing in...

Memories of the night her own happiness ended.

The night of the betrayal.

That summer, in late August, Mackenzie Daken had died, and Colby and Eleanor had come back to Canada for the funeral.

They'd been living in Australia since their wedding almost three years before, having chosen to settle there because Eleanor had wanted to be close to her widowed mother in Melbourne. Colby had started an Australian branch of Daken Construction and was doing extremely well.

Jem had attended the memorial service, but Greer—in the throes of final exams—had been unable to accompany her. Right after the exams were over, she had driven up to the lake with Jem, and didn't come into contact with Colby till he and Eleanor turned up a week later; the couple planned to spend a few days there, readying the Daken cottage for sale.

For Greer, seeing Colby again was a taste of heaven, but she made sure she showed no sign to anyone that she was in love with him. Brad Pierson had come to the cottage for a few days, too; Lisa was carrying their third child, and it wasn't due till October, but she'd been threatening to miscarry, so her doctor had hospitalized her. Brad's mother was taking care of his two daughters,

Brittany and Sarah, and Brad—stressed out with worry over Lisa, and with problems at work to boot—had taken some time off to relax.

That Colby was as besotted as ever with Eleanor was plain; and because it made Greer's heart ache to watch them together, she'd spent a lot of time with Brad, laughing and joking with him much more than she normally would have, to make sure nobody suspected her real feelings.

On the third day after Colby and Eleanor arrived at the lake, Colby had gone to Toronto to meet with his father's lawyers regarding the sale of Mac's house in the city. Since the meeting was scheduled for evening, Colby planned to stay over and drive back to the cottage in the morning.

That night, Jem went to bed around eleven, leaving Greer and Eleanor sitting on the veranda at the Daken cottage, the moon lighting up the beach in a way that made it look like a silver and purple fairyland. Eleanor seemed restless, and disinclined to chat. In the end, Greer left her, and went off to bed.

But once there she couldn't sleep for the heat. She tossed and turned for almost an hour, naked, on top of the covers, but sleep still eluded her, so in the end she got up. After slipping on a bikini, she tiptoed out of her room, hoping a stroll in the night air might cool her off.

She walked along the beach just below the cottages. All three were in darkness . . . and the occupants, she guessed, all asleep—Eleanor in the Daken cottage, Jem in the Westbury cottage and Brad in his.

But after she'd gone a little way past the Pierson place, she heard an unfamiliar sound ahead. It seemed to come from the edge of the forest about ten feet away, from the black-shadowed grassy area under a large maple tree. It sounded, Greer decided with a frown, like someone crying.

She paused, listening intently. It sounded like *Eleanor*. But whatever could be wrong? Trying to decide what to do, Greer crept forward hesitantly, stopping with a shiver after she'd gone a few steps into the dark shadowy area under the tree.

For long minutes, she stood there, but heard nothing now but the whisper of the breeze in the leafy branches above her head. She had just convinced herself she'd been mistaken, when she heard the sobbing again...*very* close by. But...no, not sobbing. Moaning. Moaning that, as she stood frozen, bewilderedly peering down into the dark shadows, became more anguished, pained...a panting, desperate—

She thought she saw a shimmer of blond hair not a yard away. She was about to whisper *'Eleanor? Is that you?'* when she heard it. Heard the sound that jolted her heart against her lungs so she could scarcely breathe. A groan...

A man's groan.

And a voice. A man's voice. *Brad's* voice, rasping out words...of passion.

Then Eleanor's whisper—husky, and brittle with excitement. 'Do you like this?' There was a rustle of sound. 'Oh, I *know* you're going to like this...'

Another groan. Again a man's groan, thick, deepthroated.

And then...an escalating series of inarticulate pleas, Eleanor's whimpered 'Don't stop, oh, don't stop now...' and then a crescendo of—

Hands pressed hard against her ears in a desperate attempt to block out the horrible, the unthinkable, Greer stumbled behind the maple tree. With a stifled cry, she sank to the ground, and squeezing her eyes shut, rocked back and forth, back and forth—

'What the hell is going on in there?'

Colby's voice shattered the air. Harsh, challenging, it ripped through Greer like the jagged blade of a chain saw. For a terrifying moment, she thought he was addressing *her*. Aghast, she peeked around the tree trunk... but when she saw where he was standing on the beach, his white shirt fluorescent in the moonlight, she knew he couldn't possibly have seen her. No, he was addressing the two people who had been making love in the shadows, so close to her she could now hear their ragged breathing. He must have come walking along the beach, to stretch his legs after the long drive from Toronto—

'Pierson!' Colby's bellow almost deafened Greer. 'I can see it's you! Get out here!'

A frantic female whisper sizzled in the air then Greer heard a startled protest, swiftly cut off. Immediately after, someone brushed past her into the forest—Eleanor, light on her feet as she scrambled by in the dark, leaving behind nothing but a hint of her perfume. And then...Brad's voice, panicky, uncertain. '*Greer*— wait—'

Greer felt her heartbeats jar. Why was Brad saying her name? But as her mind reeled confusedly, she heard Colby's voice again, so harsh now it was almost unrecognizable.

'Greer, come out this minute. If you don't, by God, I'll come in and get you!'

She had never heard him so angry. Hardly knowing what she was doing, she uncoiled her body and got up unsteadily. She reached out to the tree trunk to support herself, but lost her balance. With a cry, she fell sideways against the sun-dried branches of a bush, the crackling noise echoing in the stillness, echoing and reechoing, over and over.

Colby thudded toward her, and before she could draw a breath, he had pulled her out onto the moonlit beach.

Brad had come out of his hiding place, too, right behind her, but she had no time to waste thinking of Brad. All her thoughts were centered on Colby...and when she saw the expression of revulsion on his face as he looked at her, she felt as if she was sliding down into a dark bottomless hole. It was obvious he believed she'd been the one making love with Brad...because Eleanor—with Brad's cooperation—had set it up that way.

Oh, what a sly and selfish mind her cousin had...and oh, what a swiftly manipulative one. She could have had no idea that Greer was close by; she was probably on her way now to the Westbury cottage, intent on securing Greer's cooperation in this deception. Greer knew it was in her power to wipe the look of contempt from Colby's face; knew that with a few quiet words, she could exonerate herself and regain his respect.

But even as pain twisted her heart so she almost cried out with the intensity of it, she realized that his pain would be even greater than her own, if he were to find out the truth.

'Oh, spare the tears,' he said with soft menace as his steely grip on her wrist tightened, 'spare me the tears.' His indrawn breath was harsh...his tone cruel as he said, 'Get inside! I have some things I want to...say...to Brad Pierson and you don't want to be around to hear them!'

Greer spun her blurred gaze to Brad. Would he say the words that would clear her? She could see by the evasive shift of his gaze that he would not. Oh, she was well aware that all she ought to feel for him was repugnance, but she couldn't help feeling a faint welling of pity, too. He had had his moment of pleasure, and now he'd have to pay for it. She just hoped he felt it was worth it. At least, in her own case, she knew that Colby would never lay a hand on her.

It might have been easier if he had, she'd often thought afterward; easier to bear a physical punishment—for a sin of which she was innocent—than to have to bear the contempt he heaped on her the following evening.

Physical punishment might have broken her bones, but the punishment he did inflict on her—the withdrawal of his affection and friendship—had broken her heart.

And from that, she had never recovered.

'Greer, darling, I've made a pot of tea!'

Startled back to the present, she saw Jem at the back door, and determinedly squashing her memories, she gave a quick wave, and walked along the path to join her.

'The barbecue's going to be such fun,' Jem said. 'Lisa has invited Colby, too. It'll be just like old times.'

'It will, won't it!' Greer said lightly as she tried to ignore the sudden jarring of her heartbeats. 'Except, of course, that Brad won't be there.'

'Oh, didn't Lisa mention?' Jem patted her topknot. 'Brad is coming later, in the Mercedes. He'll be here by eight.'

CHAPTER FOUR

THE WRAPAROUND veranda at the Pierson cottage was roofed, its wooden furniture painted sage green to blend in with the surrounding landscape . . . and flowers were everywhere. Orange geranium spilled from clay pots on the deck and the stairs; bowls of lupins adorned the low casual tables; and ivies, sapphire lobelia, and fuchsia trailed in profusion from hanging moss baskets suspended by hooks from the eaves.

Normally Greer would have delighted in looking at the colorful blossoms and inhaling their sweet and spicy scents, but—for her, at least—tonight was *not* normal. Her love for Colby kept threatening to spill over, and she was terrified it would show in her eyes, her voice, her body language . . . but along with that love smoldered a burning resentment at the way he was treating her, and the constant effort to control her conflicting emotions had stimulated a pain in her temples that showed no signs of letting up . . .

And now had come the moment she'd been dreading. She and Colby were alone again.

The barbecue was over. Lisa had gone inside to put on another pot of coffee. Jem had taken the children—Brittany, Sarah, Chris and Jamie—for a stroll along the beach. And Brad had phoned earlier to say he was delayed.

A tense silence had stretched out between Greer and Colby after the others had gone; now Greer stiffened when Colby finally broke that silence.

47

'So,' his voice had a cynical edge, 'have you seen old Brad lately?' Sprawled back in a lounger a few feet from where Greer was sitting, he fixed her with a hooded gaze.

'Brad?' Her own gaze was cold. 'I haven't seen him in eight years. Not since the last time I was here.'

One black eyebrow rose. 'It was just a passing fancy, then?'

Compressing her lips, Greer darted a glance toward the kitchen window, at the end of the patio. *'What are you trying to do?'* she demanded in a low angry tone.

'Don't worry.' Colby's eyes had a contemptuous glitter. 'Lisa can't hear. Would you care, anyway? My God, when I think of how she used to look out for you when you were an adolescent—going to bat for you when Jem's outdated notions would have made you different from your peers, answering all the questions you were too shy as a teenage girl to ask your grandmother—when I watched you with Lisa tonight, saw you chat and laugh with her as if you truly felt worthy of her friendship— tell you the truth, it turned my *stomach.* She's one of the best and what you did to her was unforgivable.'

'In that case,' Greer hissed, 'why are you so hell-bent on spending time with me? Why didn't you go with Jem and the kids? I expected you to. That's why I said I just wanted to sit here and—'

'Precisely. You said you wanted to sit here. And wait for Brad? Sweetheart, I wouldn't miss this meeting for the world. Then later, when the children...and Jem...have gone to bed, we can sit here and enjoy a drink together under the stars—a pleasant four-some...Lisa and Brad...you and I.'

'My reason for wanting to sit here was not so I could watch for Brad.' As Greer jerked her head furiously, her hair swung forward over her cheeks. With shaking fingers she threaded the pale strands back. 'I stayed because I wanted to be away from you. So *stop* linking us together. There'll be no "you and I", Colby. Not now, not ever.'

'You're a passionate woman, Greer—and on a warm night such as this, with wine coursing through your veins and romantic music pulsing in the air—' he was referring, of course, to the taped voice of Julio Iglesias, as tender as the most intimate caress, drifting from the kitchen window '—I'm sure sex and seduction are very much on your mind. As I told you this morning, I intend taking you to my bed at the first opportunity—'

Greer's chair legs scraped on the wooden deck as she got to her feet. 'I don't have to take this from you! Make my excuses to Lisa—'

'Shall I tell her you have a headache?' His lips slanted in a derisive smile.

'Tell her any damned thing you like!' Greer turned on her heel, but as she did, she saw that someone was coming up the steps to the veranda . . . and she came to an abrupt stop.

'Brad!' His name came out on a gasp. 'I didn't hear your car—'

If she was startled, no less was he. He halted in his tracks, a faint flush rising over his slightly irregular but not unpleasant features. Tall and solidly built—a rugger player during his university years—Brad Pierson had in high school been voted the Boy Most Likely to Succeed. He had, indeed, been successful, landing a job after university with one of Toronto's most prestigious law firms . . . and then going on to marry the senior partner's daughter, the plump but exceptionally pretty Lisa Abercrombie.

All these facts swirled around in Greer's head as she stared at the man facing her. She felt dazed, but even as Brad finally came to life, and with a forced-looking smile, came toward them, she realized Colby had got up, too, and was standing beside her. Before she could anticipate what he was going to do, he'd put an arm around her shoulder, his grip inescapable.

'Brad.' His voice was a lazy drawl. 'Long time no see. Greer and I have been sitting here reminiscing, catching up on our old friendship. Lord, it's as if we'd never been apart.' He held out his hand in greeting.

Even as she bristled under Colby's controlling grip, Greer saw Brad hesitate. Perhaps he was remembering his last meeting with Colby when Colby had given him— among other things—a black eye and a split lip. Then taking in a deep breath, Brad took the outstretched hand and shook it firmly.

'Good to see you, Colby. I had no idea you'd be here. Nor you, Greer.'

There was no mistaking the softening of his voice as he addressed her; Greer heard it, and she was sure Colby had, too. Had Colby also noticed the slight darkening of Brad's eyes as he'd looked at her—a darkening she interpreted as a sign of his remorse and guilt at the way he and Eleanor had railroaded her into covering up for her cousin on that moonlit night so many years ago?

Brad cleared his throat. 'Is... Eleanor with you?'

Colby's arm was still lying over Greer's shoulders; at Brad's question, she felt the muscles spasm, but there was no sign of any emotion in his voice as he said, 'Eleanor died six months ago. Our son is here with me. Jamie.'

Brad looked shaken. 'Good Lord, Colby... I'm sorry... I had no idea... what a helluva thing...'

To smooth over the awkward moment, Greer said, 'Jem's here, Brad. She's taken the children along the beach, to walk off the calorie-laden dessert Lisa gave us! So... tell me... how was your drive up? I expect the roads were—'

'Sweetheart,' Colby broke in silkily, 'weren't you just rushing off somewhere when Brad arrived? I'm sure he wouldn't want to keep you from... whatever was so important?'

Outraged by his rude interruption, Greer tried to jerk herself free from his grip, but he only clamped his arm more solidly around her. 'I haven't seen Brad for *years*,' she said, keeping her voice steady. 'I'd like to—'

'I think,' Colby's tone was soft, the menace in it for her ears alone, 'that what *Brad* would like is to go inside and spend some time with his wife.' His eyes had a mocking glint. 'Surely you wouldn't want to be a...gooseberry?'

Resentment was like a cord choking Greer's throat. Yet even as she struggled to keep her temper, she acknowledged that Brad must have been rocked to the core at the news of Eleanor's death, and it would be a kindness to let him have some time to himself. Fuming inside, she somehow managed to swallow her anger as Colby cleverly frog-marched her down off the deck. Once they reached the beach, just when she was going to ram her elbow into his stomach, he released her.

'Well,' he murmured, 'I managed that beautifully— Brad will assume we're a couple, and I don't think he'd ever want to be on the receiving end of my fist again, so perhaps we can have a civilized holiday here after all. What do you think, sweetheart?'

'I am not your sweetheart,' Greer snapped, 'and at the soonest opportunity, I shall make it plain to Brad that you and I are not, and never will be, a couple, and that this particular little twosome you've dreamed up has only one player. So be careful, Colby, or you're going to end up with egg all over your face.'

'Rather egg all over my face,' Colby said coolly, 'than egg all over Lisa's. Keep clear of Brad Pierson, Greer. If you don't, you'll be sorry.'

'Is that a warning...or a threat?'

'I believe,' he said, 'it was a threat.'

'There's nothing you can do to hurt me,' Greer said quietly. 'Nothing at all.' Because, she could have added, you cannot break a heart that is already broken. She slipped her hands into the pockets of her shorts, and turning from him, stared out over the lake. She could sense the pent-up emotion in him... and it was equaled only by the pent-up emotion inside herself. The tension, she decided, was unbearable, and she was going to do something about it.

She turned again, and looked up at Colby squarely. 'You know something? I've had *enough* of this squabbling. Listen to me, because I don't want to have to say this a second time. *I have no interest whatsoever in Brad Pierson.* Now, if you really meant what you said about us all having a civilized holiday, why can't we try to do just that? People are supposed to have fun when they're on vacation, right?'

He looked at her for a long moment, his eyes narrowed. Only when he heard the sound of laughter, coming from farther along the beach, did he glance away. Greer followed his gaze, and saw Jem and the children coming toward them.

'They must have walked as far as the Trillium Lodge,' Colby said. 'I'm going to meet them. Want to come?'

Greer sensed that this was as close to a truce as they were going to get, and realized that under the circumstances it was probably the best she could hope for.

'Sure,' she said, and realized with some surprise that her head was no longer pounding quite as badly.

As they walked along the beach together, Colby slowed his pace to allow her to keep up with him. Though she was over five feet six and long-legged, he had always been able to outwalk and outrun her—that was one of the many things Greer remembered about him. Only one. Her heart twisted. She also remembered that he liked his hot dogs slathered in mustard, and he preferred beer to wine. He liked to read nonfiction—mainly autobiographies and travel books. He enjoyed listening to country music, especially Hank Williams... but he also enjoyed Mozart, Domingo, Chopin and the Stones, though not necessarily in that order. He liked to swim, to fish, to ski, to hike...

And she knew, from what Eleanor had told her, that he liked to kiss.

Greer felt a slow heat burn her cheeks. Colby had never kissed her, during all those summers they'd spent at the lake...there was, after all, a seven-year difference in their ages, and to him she had always been a child.

But he had kissed her just hours ago...and if he had enjoyed it, he had shown no sign of it. In fact, if the cynical smile that had curled his lips afterward had been anything to go by, he would have found even a hot dog without mustard more palatable.

She noticed that sand was dribbling into her thongs, making the soles of her feet uncomfortable. She stopped, and took the thongs off. Colby paused, waiting for her, and when she lost her balance and reached out automatically for support, she found herself grasping his bare forearm.

The contact was as electrical as if she had caught hold of a live cable. She snatched her hand back.

'Sorry!' Her quick apology came out huskily. Flicking her gaze up as she straightened, she found Colby looking at her with a strange expression in his eyes; she couldn't read it...yet it caused her to feel a tremor of unease.

'What?' Her voice was tense.

To her surprise, the corners of his mouth tugged up in a smile...a reluctant smile, a wry smile, but nevertheless a smile. 'We did have some good times, didn't we? My God, you could be *such* a pest...and yet without you, holidays at the lake wouldn't have been the same. How many summers did we spend here together?'

Seven summers. Even in her sleep, she could have come up with the answer. The happiest summers of her life.

She threw one arm out in a purposely vague gesture. 'Five years? Or was it six! Let's see, Gran started bringing me to the cottage after Mom and Dad died, so I would have been . . . seven, that first summer—'

'And I was fourteen. Do you remember the time we watched the sunrise together, from the Sprite, in the middle of the lake? It was my birthday present to you— your tenth birthday, as I recall—and you were petrified Jem would be awake before we got back, and discover you'd snuck out in the dark. What you didn't know was that I was even more nervous than you, because if my father had known what I was up to—' He shook his head, but she thought she detected a twinkle in his eyes.

Why was he doing this to her? Taking her back to a time when their relationship had been as perfect as flawless crystal? How could she have known then that that very perfection made it all the more vulnerable?

She swung her thongs lightly, back and forth, from one hand. 'I've watched a few sunrises since then.' She hoped her airy tone would camouflage the teary emotions his words had stirred in her. 'Jem and I went to Hawaii five years ago, and watched the sun rise, on Easter Sunday, from the hill at the Punch Bowl Memorial. Now *that* is a sight I shall *never* forget!'

If Colby wanted to step back into the past, he would have to go on his own.

It was a journey that—for her—could bring only pain.

Though the walk with Jem along the beach seemed to have energized the Pierson children, it had left Jamie weary and heavy-eyed. He was dragging a little way behind the others, and didn't put up a fight when Colby said, 'Bedtime for you, my lad!' and bore him off.

'Your father's here,' Greer told the other three children, and with whoops of glee, they raced away to look for Brad.

'What a happy trio they are,' Jem said, with a sigh, as she and Greer strolled back together. 'But Jamie...oh, I can't bear to see the way he mopes. He's about the

same age as Chris, and I hoped they'd hit it off, but they
didn't. Sarah tried hard to be friendly and include him,
but the more she tried, the farther Jamie retreated into
his shell. I do hope she won't give up on him.'

'Sarah...she's the younger daughter, isn't she?'

'Mmm. She's ten, and a sweet child...takes after her
mother. Brittany is almost thirteen...and like her father
in many ways. She has a good heart, but sometimes she
can be impulsive...careless. Sarah adores her, but Sarah's
very sensitive, and I know it hurts her when Brittany is
unkind.'

'You watch everyone, don't you!' Greer remarked with
an amused smile. 'Not much gets by my Gran!'

Jem flicked a hank of weeds aside with the tip of her
cane. 'Those two—Brittany and Sarah—sometimes
remind me of Eleanor and you. Eleanor...well, let's just
say she also could be...careless, while you were the most
sensitive little girl I've ever known.'

Moved by the affection in her grandmother's eyes,
Greer felt her cheeks turn warm. 'I was sensitive, all
right,' she said lightly. 'Cried at the drop of a hat, didn't
I!'

'Yes, you tended to cry when things hurt you. But I'd
never seen you cry the way you cried that night down
by the water,' she added softly, 'the last time you were
here. And you never did tell me why you were so mis-
erable. I had my suspicions, of course, but I didn't press
you at the time.'

'Thank you for that, Gran,' Greer said, trying not to
flinch before her grandmother's searching gaze. What a
mistake it had been to come back to the lake! she thought
despairingly. First of all Colby was trying to rake up old
memories...now her grandmother seemed determined
to probe into places where probing was not bearable.
'But it's all so long ago. I've put it behind me and...I
don't like talking about that stuff. It's ancient history.

'Now tell me—' she somehow managed a cheerful smile '—you went as far as the Trillium Lodge—did the dining room look as inviting from the beach as it used to—the linen tableclothes, the sparkling silver and glassware, the waitresses gliding around in their black-and-white uniforms? I used to think how exciting it would be to book in for dinner one night!'

Jem patted Greer's hand. 'Yes, dear, it looked very inviting. And I was thinking, funnily enough, that you and I should go along there for a meal one evening...pamper ourselves with some real French cuisine. Let's do it...next weekend—it'll be something to look forward to.'

Next weekend. Greer felt as if her heart had turned into a heavy lump in her chest. No *way* was she going to come back to the lake next weekend. Thank heavens she had several days to come up with some good reason why it would be impossible to leave the city...

'Saturday night,' her grandmother was murmuring, 'would be best...'

'Gran...are you going back to Lisa's for a while?'

'Mmm, I'll drop by and have a chat with Brad. I haven't seen him since last summer. Does he know about Eleanor?'

'Yes. Colby told him.'

'That would have been a shock.'

'Yes, he was really upset. Gran, would you make my excuses to Lisa? Tell her I've...had a busy week and I need an early night.'

'Are you feeling all right? You do look pale.'

'I had a headache earlier but it's gone now...I'm just not in the mood for small talk.' They had come alongside the Westbury cottage. 'Good night, Gran.' Greer gave her grandmother a quick hug. 'I'll see you in the morning.'

'Good night, Greer. Sleep well.'

Tucking her hands into the pockets of her shorts, Greer veered off toward the cottage, thankful Jem hadn't tried to dissuade her from going in. And she hadn't lied—she *had* had a busy week, and she could do with an early night.

The point was...would she be able to sleep, knowing that Colby would be sitting on the Pierson's veranda, less than forty feet away?

Surprisingly she drifted off to sleep within minutes, only to come sharply awake again, sometime later.

Moonlight dappled the bedroom, and when she reached for her watch, she saw that it was almost four o'clock.

What had roused her? Was her grandmother up and moving around? Perhaps she wasn't feeling well...

Swinging her legs over the edge of the bed, Greer crossed to her door, and opening it, crept along the shadowy lobby. Jem always slept with her door ajar, and even before Greer peeked into the moonlit room and saw her grandmother lying there safely, she heard her snoring, the sound soft and gently vibrating, like the purr of a contented kitten.

Smiling, Greer padded barefoot through to the kitchen, tugging up the spaghetti strap of her black silk nightie as it caught on the curve of her upper arm.

Whatever had wakened her, she knew it couldn't have been Gran, but now that she was up, she felt as wide-awake as an owl on sentry duty, and she knew from experience that there was no point in going back to bed. Not yet.

The lake had never looked more beautiful, she mused as she glanced out the kitchen window; its surface gleamed in the moonlight like pewter. She grasped the edges of the sink, and as she savored the stillness of the night, she felt it call out to the most primal corner of her being.

Irresistibly drawn, she went out onto the deck, down the steps leading onto the lawn and onto the beach. She walked slowly out along the jetty, feeling the gentle dip and rise of the floating structure under her bare feet...and once at the end, she curled her fingers around the smooth top bar of the railing, and looked out over the lake.

It wasn't as quiet on the jetty as it was ashore; here the water lapped against the pilings, slapping and splashing—almost, Greer thought with a smile, as if someone was swimming in the shadowy depths, flipping around—

She gasped and cried out, as all of a sudden a figure rose out of the water right where she was peering—but even as her shriek echoed back at her, she heard a mocking laugh.

'Sorry if I startled you...but believe me, seeing you standing peering down just now startled me just as much!'

With a great flurry of foam, Colby pulled himself up out of the lake, and onto the dock. Standing straight, he shook his head and then drew a hand through it, scattering cold droplets over Greer's bare shoulders as he did.

'Hey, watch it!' she protested, her voice breathless, her heart still pounding from the shock of his sudden appearance. 'I didn't come out here for a cold shower!'

He looked like some magnificent rainwashed bronzed statue, she thought as she took a step back. But unlike a statue, he wasn't inanimate; she could tell from the glint in his eyes that he was seeing and appreciating every inch of flesh revealed by the skimpiness of her black nightie.

He himself was wearing even less: trunks that were pale in color—hard to tell in the moonlight if they were icy blue or gray—and designed to do little other than preserve the minimum modicum of decency. Greer felt prickles of awareness dance over her skin in a way that alarmed her.

'What on earth are you doing out here in the middle of the night?' she asked haughtily.

His laugh was like a velvet finger stroking its way down her spine. 'I'm not doing anything,' he said, 'at least, not yet.' The intimation in his tone was that when he did do something, that something would involve her. He leaned back lazily against the end railing, arms folded, ankles crossed. 'Why did *you* come out?'

'Something woke me, and I knew I'd never get back to sleep so I decided to get some air. It was nice and peaceful . . . till you came on the scene.'

'It could still be nice and peaceful.' Amusement lurked around the edge of his voice. 'Or . . . something more exciting, if you feel up to it?'

'I think not,' she said tersely. 'Excitement is the last thing I need when I'm wound up and can't sleep.'

'They say sex is a great stress reliever.'

'I didn't say I was stressed—'

'Stressed, wound up . . . same difference. Sex'll cure it every time.'

'How like a man, to promote sex as the cure. Wouldn't hot milk and an aspirin do the trick just as well?'

'Come here.'

'What . . . ?'

His hand snaked out and he pulled her toward him. Not so close that she was touching his wet flesh . . . but close enough. Too close. Greer felt as if something was blocking her throat. She swallowed, and made a jerky attempt to regain possession of her hand, but he only caught the other and held the two together, in one of his. His eyes were a disturbing mixture of dark and bright; dark with intent, bright with deviltry.

'What . . . what are you doing?' Greer's voice sounded thick and unfamiliar.

Colby's ominous chuckle sent a shiver of apprehension skittering over her skin. 'It's a test,' he murmured, 'so please pay attention.' He bent over and captured one of her nightie's straps with his teeth. She gasped and tried to twist away, but Colby tightened his grip.

'I'm not finished yet,' he said, through his teeth, and then maneuvered the strap over her shoulder and down her arm to her elbow. The yoke of the nightie collapsed in an ebony slither, its path halted by the swell of her breasts.

'I want you to tell me—' Colby's lips caressed the strip of pale skin between the folds of silk and her tan line, his tantalizing touch making Greer inhale a sharp breath '—if you like this—' he nudged the sheer fabric down with his mouth and the teasing forays with his tongue created a whiplash of desire that had Greer arching her head back and stifling a moan '—and this.' As she shuddered, he brushed his lips over the film of black silk shrouding the tip of her breast, the shockingly intimate caress sending her hurtling, mindless and ecstatic, into a sensual paradise...

'Do you?' His voice seemed to come from far away, through a fog of delirium. 'Do you...like this?'

An inarticulate sound of pleasure came from between Greer's lips, but even as it echoed in her ears, Colby released his grip, dropped his hands, took a step back.

She stared at him dazedly.

'I take it,' he said with an arrogant smile, 'that your response indicated a yes.' Tugging up the strap, he patted the yoke of her nightie impersonally into place, and added, in the brisk voice a doctor might use to a patient,

'So...what's it to be, Greer. Your choice—sex, of which I've just given you a taste, or hot milk and aspirin.'

For a long moment, Greer felt only confusion. But when what he had done sank in, she felt an outrage so intense it was all she could do not to kick him in the groin. She wanted to scream, she wanted to thump his chest with her fists, she wanted to stamp her feet, tear her hair, tear his hair... tear anyone's hair! Instead, gathering up every particle of self-control she possessed, she curved her lips in what she hoped would pass for a lazy, amused smile.

'Sex has a lot going for it, Colby, but I think I'll settle for aspirin and hot milk. It was an interesting test, though, and your moves were practiced and skillful. I got the impression you've used them many times before.'

'But never with quite such satisfactory results. Bodes well for when we do finally get into bed together.'

'Dream on!' she said derisively. 'Now let me pass, I want to go in.'

'Before you go—'

'Yes?' Irritably she paused as he blocked her way.

'Have you made up your mind about keeping on your grandmother's cottage?'

Greer fought to contain a hysterical laugh. How could he bring himself down to earth so quickly, when she— despite the antagonism he roused in her—still felt suspended halfway to paradise? Yet... she had to admit she did want to come to some decision regarding the cottage, and though this was certainly not the occasion she'd have chosen for such a discussion with Colby, it would be foolish to turn down the opportunity to find out what *his* plans were.

'I was wondering about the Daken cottage,' she said, avoiding a direct answer. 'Are you planning to come back here again, or is this a one-shot deal?'

'I'm seriously considering moving back to Toronto. If I decide to stay, then I shall keep the cottage, but I'd have to do a bit of renovating. As you may know, it's been rented out for the past several years and though it's been well enough maintained by the firm I hired to look after the property, it needs modernizing. I'd also add a couple of rooms.'

'So what was good enough for your father isn't good enough for you anymore?'

'We have to move with the times, Greer. Let's face it, the three cottages at this end of the lake are picturesque as all get out...but besides being small, they're habitable only in the warm weather. I'd want a winterized place, one Jamie and I could enjoy year-round. I'd want him to experience things he's never experienced before—ice fishing, snowmobiling, cross-country skiing...'

'You could rough it in the winter, as you and your father did,' Greer said, adding with a mocking edge, 'Or has life down under made you soft?'

'No, it hasn't made me soft,' Colby retorted. 'But if we vacation at the cottage, I'd want to bring Jamie's nanny with us.'

Greer blinked. 'Jamie has a nanny?'

'Not yet, but I plan to hire one. On a permanent basis.'

'But...if you marry again—'

'I don't intend to marry again.'

Greer was taken aback by the vehemence of his tone, yet...it wasn't surprising, in view of the way he'd felt about his wife. Eleanor had been the only one for him, Colby had told Greer that many times that long-ago summer...but he was only thirty-two; surely he didn't intend to spend the rest of his life in mourning? She frowned. 'Have you considered the possibility that you may fall in love again?'

'Love is the last thing I'm looking for. Once I have a nanny in place, I'll be making another...arrangement.'

'An arrangement?'

'A mistress,' he said. 'What more could a single father want? A nanny to help look after his child...and a mistress to see to his other...needs.'

Greer stared at him disbelievingly. 'You can't be serious! I don't know when I've heard of anything so—'

'Heartless? It'll be a business arrangement, Greer. And there are loads of women out there who would jump at the opportunity to be my mistress, women delighted to accept what I'm willing to offer... and the one thing I will not be offering will be my heart.' His smile was not a pleasant one. 'I won't have to take anyone by force.'

'No, of course you won't,' she managed to say in a cold voice. 'You're everything a... mistress could want.'

'You think so? I wonder then... would you be interested in the job?' He raised his eyebrows mockingly. 'You did say you aren't planning on marrying... and you have all the right... qualifications...'

'I'd rather roast in hell than be your mistress, Colby Daken!'

She shoved past him roughly and stomped her way back along the jetty, hoping that with every single nuance of her bearing, she was sending him the message that her outrage was equaled only by her disgust.

The only problem was that because of the bobbing of the wooden structure, she tripped when she was halfway along and almost fell flat on her face. As she righted herself just in time, she heard a sound from behind. A sound that reached her over the furious hammering of her heart, and over the *slip-slap* of the wavelets against the pilings.

Colby Daken was laughing at her.

And it made her so mad she could have spit nails.

CHAPTER FIVE

BRAD turned up next morning, when Greer and Jem were in the kitchen, finishing their breakfast. He declined Jem's invitation to have a cup of coffee.

'I just want a quick word with you, Jem,' he said. 'I was wondering if you could do me a couple of favors.'

'Of course,' Jem said. 'If I can.'

'It's Lisa's birthday next Saturday, and I'd like to throw a surprise party for her—just us cottage folks.'

'Oh, what fun!' Jem clapped her hands. 'What would you like me to do, Brad?'

'I plan on bringing the party food up here on Friday night in a cooler—tucked away in the back of my trunk so Lisa won't see it—and I wondered if you could make room in your fridge for it till Saturday night.'

'Sure, I have oodles of space. What else?'

'Could you get Lisa out of the way about an hour before the party—perhaps take her for a walk along the beach, with the children—then while the coast is clear, Greer and I can move the food from your kitchen over to our deck, and set everything up. Greer, are you game?'

Greer started, and looked at Brad blankly; he, like her grandmother, was assuming she was coming back to the lake next weekend, while she had already made up her mind she was going to keep herself as far from Colby Daken as she possibly could. But even as she opened her mouth to make her apologies, she saw the bright expectant look in Jem's eyes, and she felt a sinking sensation spiraling to her toes.

She cleared her throat. 'Oh, sure, I'll help any way I can. Have you told the children?'

'No, too risky—I'm not even going to tell Colby till the last minute—the fewer people who know, the better.'

'But what if Colby makes other plans? What if he's not going to be here?' Jem's tone was concerned.

'He mentioned last night that he's having some lumber delivered next Saturday afternoon—he's planning to do some repairs to the boathouse—and he asked if I'd be around later to help with some lifting.'

'So... you're all set!' Jem looked pleased.

And Greer smiled, to give the impression the prospect of the party was one she found pleasurable, too, when in fact she would have found it infinitely more pleasurable to have spent the following weekend in her apartment, holed up with a couple of videos, the latest *New York Times* bestseller, and a bottle of chilled white wine.

'Thanks,' Brad said, 'I really appreciate your help.'

'It's given us something to look forward to!' Jem said. 'And now... I'm going to do a bit of weeding, before the sun gets round to the flower beds.' Scooping up her cane, she crossed the kitchen and went out into the hallway.

As the screen door at the back of the cottage creaked shut behind her, Brad's smile faded, and he looked at Greer with an expression that made her senses twitch warily.

'Brad,' she said quickly, 'I really don't want to talk about—'

'I know, and I don't, either. But I think we have to, if only to clear the air. Greer, I've gone through hell, the past years, because of what Eleanor and I did—'

'Since you insist on talking about it, then I'll tell you, Bradley Pierson, you must have been out of your mind to betray Lisa. If she knew, it would break her heart—'

'She does know.' Brad's voice was steady. 'I told her. Oh, not right away. I waited till after Chris was some months old, and Lisa had regained her strength. And you're right. It did break her heart. But she loved me, and she had faith in me. She knew it would never happen again. Not with Eleanor. Not with anybody.' He inhaled a shaky breath. 'God knows I didn't deserve her forgiveness, but she gave me it, and I accepted it.'

'Brad, how could you have let it *happen?*'

'You want to know how it happened?' Brad's features were grim. 'I'll tell you. I'd gone for a stroll—I had no idea Eleanor had followed me till I got to the end of the beach. We stood and chatted there for a few minutes, but she started coming on to me. I didn't realize it at first, but then she started fiddling with the buttons of her beach top...opening them, one at a time, and watching me all the while from under those long thick lashes of hers—I got the crazy feeling she was doing some kind of a striptease. I told her I was going back, it was getting late. She laughed, that soft sexy chuckle she had...and then she slipped off the top. She was naked underneath. Stark.'

Greer gasped. 'Oh, Brad—'

'I have no excuses for what happened...and I offered none to Lisa. It takes two to tango...and I tangoed.' He made a brusque gesture. 'But my relationship with Lisa isn't what I set out to talk to you about. I just wanted to let you know that ever since that night, I've felt guilty as hell that you were the scapegoat, and Colby was left unaware of the truth.'

'Water under the bridge, Brad—'

'When Eleanor fled after telling me to make it seem as if I was with you, I should have come clean right then. But I hesitated, and then of course Colby lit into me and I staggered back to the cottage punch-drunk. In the morning, I was just so damned ashamed of myself I took off—'

'I saw you leave, remember?' Greer's voice was strained. 'I was out front when you drove away. You looked as if you'd been in a bar-room brawl.'

'Yes, I remember. How could I forget? Your face was so white and your expression so anguished—'

'It was a bad time.' Greer turned away and stared dully out the window. She heard Brad come up behind her.

'You could have cleared yourself,' he murmured. 'If not on the beach that night, then the following day. But I gather, from the way Colby's been treating you, that you never did. Why on earth not?'

Greer sighed. 'To protect him, of course. He was so in love with Eleanor, it would have devastated him to learn she'd been unfaithful. I think I'd have done anything, said anything, to keep him from being hurt.'

'But Eleanor's dead now, Greer—there's no need to keep the truth a secret any longer. Colby *must* be told... and if you won't tell him, I shall.'

She whirled around, her eyes wide with horror. 'No! You mustn't!'

'But—'

'Eleanor's dead, yes. But her memory is all Colby has left of her. *Nothing* must be allowed to tarnish that! *Nothing!* Do you understand?'

Brad frowned, opened his mouth as if to protest and then closed it again. In the end he nodded, but slowly, his acquiescence obviously reluctantly given. His eyes, as he looked deeply into Greer's, were dark with regret... regret mingled with compassion. 'The guy always had such a soft spot for you. And you were in love with him, weren't you?'

'You lawyers really know how to get at the truth, don't you? What should I say in answer to that... something about the Fifth Amendment—' Greer's voice caught on a sob.

'Oh, honey...'

Brad drew her comfortingly into his arms . . . and after a tense moment of resistance, she felt her body slump. Slump in despair. Of course she'd been in love with Colby. And, she acknowledged miserably, she still was. But he would never see her except as a woman who had slept with a married man. A woman without morals. A woman he could never trust.

Her pain was ragged; barbed wire tearing through her heart. 'Oh, Brad,' she whispered, 'love is hell—'

A movement by the kitchen's screen door caught her eye, and as she blinked back her tears, she saw a tall figure standing outside. Watching. His lean face distorted with anger. His shoulders taut with barely controlled emotion.

Colby.

What was he doing here?

But before she could come up with an answer, her nemesis tore open the screen door and slammed it savagely back so that it hit the outside wall with a crash.

Brad swung around, an arm still embracing Greer.

'Colby? What the—?'

'Your *wife* sent me to bring you home for breakfast. You do *remember* you have a wife?' Colby's eyes burned with a glittering fire. 'What the *hell* are you waiting for?' he snarled as Brad hesitated. 'Get your butt *out* of here!'

In the tension-packed silence, Greer heard Lisa's voice drifting through the air from somewhere outside. 'Colby, your breakfast's on the table. Did you find Brad?'

Colby's face was an ugly red, anger bulging in every vein. '*Git!*' He jerked his head violently in the direction of the open doorway as he stared at Brad, and Brad, whose face was white with strain, gave Greer's arm a quick squeeze before he shouldered roughly past Colby and stormed away.

'Coming, hon,' Greer heard him call. 'Be right there.'

Colby now directed his rage toward Greer. She stiffened as he came toward her menacingly, looking as if he wanted to grab her and shake her till her teeth fell out.

She stepped back.

'Too bad you've already got a breakfast invitation,' she said brightly. 'I'd have offered you a cup of coffee!'

Swiveling on her heel, she took off along the hallway and into her bedroom, where she slammed the door. She knew Colby wouldn't follow her there, in case Jem was around.

Breathlessly she crossed to the window, and skulked behind the curtain. In a moment she saw him march across the lawn toward the trees and shrubs separating the two cottages. There was no sign of Brad; no sign of Lisa. And though she couldn't see Sarah, she heard the child's voice.

'Oh, *there* you are, Mr. Daken—come on, breakfast's ready. If you don't hurry, all the waffles will be gone!'

Greer drew back and sank onto the edge of her bed, shaking. What quirk of fate had brought Colby to the kitchen door at precisely the moment she'd been lolling in Brad's arms? Was it some bad karma come back to haunt her?

Oh, what did it matter? Colby's opinion of her could hardly get any lower than it already was.

And that was rock bottom.

After washing the breakfast dishes, Greer changed into her bikini, and ran down to the beach. She swam for quarter of an hour, and then made for the float anchored a half mile from the shore. After she hauled herself up, she wrung the water from her ponytail and lay down on her stomach, her brow resting on the back of her entwined fingers.

She let her body follow the subtle swaying of the float, and in time found that the motion, along with the growing heat of the sun's rays on her back, was seducing her into a lethargic state.

It was amazing how the lilt of water and the radiance of heat could banish stress. Colby Daken seemed, at this moment, a million miles away—

The float suddenly dipped to one side, and Greer glanced round. She saw a man's hand grasping the raised edge, a wet dark head surging from the water, and a second later realized with dismay that the intruder was Colby.

She stifled a frustrated exclamation and settled her brow on her hands again. Damn! Couldn't the man leave her alone? She sensed him looking at her, felt cool drops prickling her skin and imagined him shaking the water from his hair...and then she heard a rustle of movement, followed by a scuffling sound, another movement of the float. What was he doing? Was he glaring at her, furious because she seemed relaxed?

Tensely she waited for him to castigate her for trying to seduce Brad...because of course that was how he had interpreted the little scene he'd come on in the kitchen...

But he said nothing.

And after several long minutes of lying there, hardly breathing, Greer could bear the suspense no longer. *If you've got something to say,* she wanted to scream, *say it and get it over with.*

But still he said nothing. Finally, with her heart thudding like a hammer against her ribs, she carefully turned her head and peeked over the curve of her arm.

He was there all right, but no longer standing. He was lying not more than two feet away, on his back. His hands were clasped comfortably behind his head...

And he was asleep.

Eyes closed, black lashes a charcoal sweep shadowing his hard cheekbones, and lips very slightly parted, he was issuing a barely audible snoring sound.

In sleep, Greer decided with a feeling of despair, he was even more irresistible than he was when he was awake...

And oh, how she wanted to touch him.

Her fingers itched to trace a path over his hair-roughened chest; to tease one soft nut brown nipple till it hardened; to draw a palm down over the flat belly, follow the arrowing invitation of dark hair to his navy trunks; to slip her fingertips beneath the waistband and follow that intriguing arrow to its destination—

'Be my guest.'

Greer's breath caught with a strangled sound. She snatched her gaze from his trunks—the wet fabric revealing more than any fabric had a right to reveal, provoking responses that no modest maiden would properly acknowledge—and stared, horrified, at Colby. He was regarding her with a knowing expression that made her heartbeats stagger in one fell swoop from temporary paralysis to a tempo that resembled the out-of-control hurtle of a runaway truck.

A logging truck.

Fully loaded.

'I don't mind,' he murmured, a malicious glint in the depths of his hooded blue eyes, 'I really don't.'

'Don't mind...what?' Greer felt as if she was forcing her words through wadded cotton wool.

'I don't mind if you...touch me.' Black eyebrows rose cynically. 'That's what you want to do, isn't it?'

'Why?' She sounded as if she was choking. 'Why...would I want to touch you?'

The corners of his lips twitched in the beginnings of a smile. 'The same reason people want to climb Everest. Because it's there.' He let the smile loosen...and Greer felt as if her blood had been replaced by sweet, dark melted treacle. She had never been able to resist Colby's smile...

But why was he smiling at her? Why wasn't he tearing her off a strip for having been in Brad's arms? What was he up to?

Panic tumbled through her. *I've got to get out of here,* she decided . . . but even as she made the decision, Colby tugged the hand closest to him from under her cheek, and braided their fingers firmly, inescapably, together.

'Here,' he said softly, 'allow me to be your guide.'

'Guide?' Her voice was faint.

His eyes had become cloudy, and as she saw the simmering desire in the hazy depths, the temperature of her blood soared again; her body felt as if it was on fire.

Feeling totally helpless, she allowed him to lift her hand and press it against his chest. She could feel the impression of each separate black hair on her palm and it was with a severe jolt of her pulse that she realized that the tip of her middle finger was resting exactly where she'd wished it moments ago . . . and was tightening the soft skin to a tight bud exactly as she'd imagined it doing moments ago.

If she'd felt hot before, now she felt as if she was being consumed by fire.

'Are you crazy!' she hissed, no longer lying prone but twisted on her side, facing him, her body supported by her right elbow. 'We can be seen from the beach!'

'So? What's to see? All we're doing is lying here, with your arm draped casually over my chest—'

'There's nothing casual about the way my arm is draped over your chest!' Greer flared, trying unsuccessfully to free her hand. 'And draping implies that the action is voluntary. It's far from that!'

'Really? But weren't you following this path—' his grip tightened further and he drew her hand down over his ribs, and on past his waist, to the muscled flatness of his belly, where he paused '—with your eyes?'

'A cat can look at a king—it doesn't follow that the cat has any desire to paw the king's torso!'

'True.' Maddeningly Colby's tone was light and amused. 'But you did want to get your pretty paws on me, didn't you? No, don't try to deny it—you're not the first woman to look at me that way...and let's face it, since I'm planning to have you in my bed by summer's end, the fact that you find me physically attractive will make our lovemaking all the more satisfying to me. I'm not one of those men who get their kicks out of forcing a reluctant woman to surrender to their advances. I get my thrills from a female who is warm, and willing...and...like you...adventurous.'

Greer gasped as he guided her hand down over his belly. With a jerk, she tried to wrench her hand free, but all she succeeded in doing was stimulate a low rumble of laughter in Colby's chest. And then, as hysteria and rage and—no use in denying it—sexual excitement clashed and roiled inside her, he released her hand.

For a mindless moment, she felt paralyzed. Her hand lay where he'd dropped it, splayed over his low-slung navy trunks, his flesh separated from the pads of her fingertips by a sleek sheath of damp fabric. Silk, she thought dizzily; a mixture of silk and some stretchy material. Perhaps Spandex—

Reality blasted through her with a force that sucked the breath from her lungs. She snatched her hand up and leaped to her feet...to find Colby staring up at her lazily.

'Old Brad got an eyeful just now.' His tone was that of a man who was smug and deeply satisfied. 'You didn't notice him, over there by the boathouse? Ah, well, no matter. He's gone now, but I'm sure he has finally got the message...hands off, if he knows what's good for him.'

Breasts heaving, Greer glared down at Colby. He had done it to her again. It had all been a game, and she had fallen for it, hook, line and sinker.

'I can't believe I used to like you,' she spat at him.
'Boy, was I *ever* dumb!'

Colby sprang to his feet and faced her, his eyes dark
and unsmiling. 'Two people don't need to like each other
to be good in bed together. And you and I are going to
be good in bed together, *very* good. Tell me I'm wrong.'

Greer felt as if her world was collapsing all around
her. She knew she should tell Colby he was wrong, but
she just couldn't say the words. She was well aware that
if he hadn't let her hand go, if he'd kept her fingers in
his and guided them down those last few inches, for her
there would have been no drawing back. Right there on
the old float, visible to Brad and anyone else who happened to be looking, she would have surrendered, with
total and wanton abandon, to his lovemaking.

Colby's soft laugh broke into her thoughts and when
she saw the arrogant curl of his lip, she realized he knew,
only too well, what she'd been thinking.

Irately she stalked to the edge of the float and dived
into the lake. But though the water out here was cool,
it did nothing to cool her anger ... or her desire, and as
she made for the shore, she knew she had to get away
from Colby. Instead of leaving in the early evening, she
would go midafternoon. The situation here was absolutely intolerable.

She'd have to come back next weekend for the surprise party, but after that, she'd keep away as much as
she could. And with a bit of luck, the man would decide
by summer's end that he was going back to Australia.
For good.

And if he didn't, she would have no option but to tell
Jem she didn't want the cottage after all.

'Brad told me he talked with you this morning.'

Greer had been leaning casually against the railing of
the Piersons's deck; at Lisa's words, she straightened,
and feeling her palms suddenly damp, slipped them into

the pockets of her linen pants. 'Yes,' she said, 'he did...and I'm glad that whole mess is behind us.'

'But it's not really over, is it! Oh, for Brad and me, it's over...but for you, it's not. Honey, I knew when you were fourteen you had a crush on Colby, and I guessed you were heartbroken when he fell for Eleanor. Now don't get me wrong, I adore Colby, he and I clicked from the very first moment we met—kindred spirits, he used to say, despite my being a few years older—but men can be so *stupid* sometimes where women are concerned—they can't see behind the glitter and the glamour—'

'Lisa, I really don't want to talk about—'

'I know, but...Greer, if there's anything Brad and I can to do help, anytime, please don't hesitate to ask.'

'Thanks, Lisa...but in this situation, there's nothing anyone can do. Your summer friendship was very important to me when I was an adolescent—you were always there for me, when I needed you—and it's wonderful that we've picked up that friendship again. But I'm all grown up now, and I have to stand on my own two feet.' Greer pushed up the cuff of her silk blouse and glanced at her watch. 'I'd better be off.' She softened her words with a smile. 'I don't want to be too late getting back.'

'Have a safe trip, then, and I'll tell Brad and the kids goodbye for you.' She bit her lip. 'Have you...told Colby you're leaving? He's in the boathouse. I saw him go over there after Jamie left to go fishing with my gang.'

'Colby and I have nothing to say to one another.'

'Honey, I know it must hurt you terribly, Colby treating you the way he does, but try to understand how he feels. We were all of us such good friends, and he believes you betrayed the trust that true friends share. Besides, he loved your sweetness and your innocence—can you imagine how disillusioned he must have been when he thought you were having a fling with a married man? Give him a chance. Go to the boathouse and say goodbye. You've nothing to lose!'

Nothing to lose.

'There's no point. Colby—oh, he makes me so mad—' Greer's voice broke '—he *still* believes there's something going on between Brad and me.'

'Why don't you just give him time—time to get used to seeing us all together again, time to get to know you again, time to see the way things *really* are?' Lisa looped an arm through one of Greer's and led her to the veranda steps. 'I think Colby's a very confused man at the moment. I happened to look out the window this morning when you were swimming in from the float— he stood staring after you, and I don't know when I've ever seen a man look so wretched.' She gave Greer a gentle push. 'Go. Say goodbye.'

Greer walked slowly down the steps, and when she got to the bottom, she hesitated. To go... or not to go—

She heard a door shut up above, and knew Lisa had gone back inside. No one was watching, to see whether or not she went to Colby. Her weekend bag was already in the car, she'd already said goodbye to Jem...

Taking in a deep breath, she started walking... along the beach toward the boathouse.

But even as she went, she could hardly believe that she was going to look for Colby. Why was she, then? Was it just because of Lisa's gentle urgings?

No, she knew full well it wasn't only that. Despite Colby's hostility toward her, despite his contempt... and despite the fact that she'd told him, just hours before, that she didn't even like him, she just had to see him one more time, before she left for home.

Weak, foolish, besotted.

That was what she was. Colby had stolen her heart and she had never been able to get it back. Love, she reflected bitterly, was a pain.

The boathouse was situated at the very end of the secluded bay on which the three cottages stood. Built with Shaker simplicity in the late 1800s, it had a steep cedar-shake roof, and white-painted board-and-batten siding.

The door lay open, and as Greer stepped inside, the sloshing of wavelets against the walls drowned out the sound of her rubber-soled shoes on the rough-planked walkway. Colby's boat, the *Summer Sprite*, swayed gently in the dark water... and Colby was nowhere to be seen.

Relief and disappointment mixed sourly inside her, and it was with a murmur of frustration that she turned to leave... but as she did, she heard a sound from the floor above, and her heartbeats stumbled.

Colby was upstairs, in the loft.

Glancing down at her cream slacks and pale blue blouse, she hesitated. The loft would be filthy, dusty, cobwebby. She had just showered. Frowning, she flicked back her hair. Then, making up her mind, with a grimace she started up the flight of narrow steps set against the wall.

The loft was a square open area, with one huge windowed wall looking out over the lake. The room was just as dirty as Greer had expected it to be... the planked floor thick with dust, the drywall dingy, the rafters festooned with cobwebs. Colby was standing at the window with his back to her, his hands in the pockets of his baggy drawstring pants, and he appeared to be lost in thought.

Greer was about to move forward and make her presence known when she noticed, among the debris scattered on the floor at her feet, a yellowed sheet of paper. The sketch on it looked familiar. She picked up the brittle sheet and saw she was right; this was her own work, a sketch she'd made one rainy afternoon when she was twelve or thirteen.

Colby's father had allowed her the run of the boathouse, and the loft had been her favorite place. She'd wistfully imagined it as the perfect setting for a honeymoon...before she'd ever had more than a glimmer of knowledge of what a honeymoon was all about! She'd drawn this detailed floor plan, with a bedroom, and en-suite bathroom; and she had chosen colors, patterns, furniture.

Colby had come on her when she'd been sitting on the wide windowsill, her mind a million miles away, and when he'd asked what she was up to, she'd said in a dreamy voice, 'Wouldn't this be a *wonderful* spot for a honeymoon? You could set the bed facing the window, and at night you could gaze at the lake, and the stars, and the moon, and feel you were the only two people in the world!'

His grin had been teasing. 'You think that's what honeymooners do? Spend their time looking out windows?'

Yes, at that time she had thought they would. What an innocent she'd been! With a shake of her head, she let the yellowed paper drift to the floor, where it settled with a rustle. The sound was faint, but Colby must have heard it.

He turned, and took his hands out of his pockets. His eyes darkened as he looked her over.

'So...' his voice, as soft as an intimate caress, had the hair at her nape rising in response '...what have we here?'

'I came to say goodbye.'

'You came to say goodbye.' He walked slowly across the loft, and when he was close, he leaned one wide shoulder lazily against the grimy wall. Sweeping a mocking gaze over her sleek designer slacks and silk shirt, he said, in a cool voice, 'So, city lady, you're off.'

Greer couldn't bear to see the hostile look in his eyes, but she forced herself to meet his gaze steadily. 'You're going to be doing some work on the boathouse?'

'Yes, down below. Brad told you?'

'Well—'

'It had to be Brad.' His voice had become hard. 'I mentioned it to no one else.'

'Yes.' Greer felt herself crumple inside as his antagonism battered her spirit. 'It was Brad.'

'Why did you come here?' The question was tersely uttered.

'Lisa thought I ought to say goodbye.'

'But why did you come?' he persisted, his tone almost angry. 'I don't see anyone with a gun at your back!'

She knew now that she could give Colby a thousand chances to get to know her again but he wouldn't take them. He wasn't interested in starting over.

'It was obviously a mistake!' She spat out the words and turned toward the stairs, but Colby shot out a hand and pulled her roughly against him. Her face was inches from his chest. He was wearing no shirt, and she could see the beads of sweat on his skin, could smell the musky scent of his body...and a rope of fire whipped deep inside her, its snaking tip flaming straight to her core. Oh, Lord, she thought desperately, I've got to get out of here...

'You've already made more than your share of mistakes,' he said softly, 'but you made one helluva mistake when you decided to pay me this little visit. Your timing couldn't have been worse...from your point of view that is. From mine, it couldn't have been better. I'd been thinking about you, you see...thinking about making love to you.'

Her shaky whimper was drowned out as he swung her around smoothly and held her against the wall. Heartbeats staggering, Greer looked dazedly up into his face.

'Thinking,' he went on huskily, 'about kissing you.'

Mind spinning, she ran the tip of her tongue over her mouth. Colby's eyes were caught by the slight movement, his gaze dropped and she knew she'd made another mistake. He'd taken it as an invitation.

With a low mutter, he drove his fingers through her hair and claimed her parted lips in an open kiss, sensual and seductive. He stroked his tongue along the length of hers, and the sheer intimacy of the caress sent excitement shuddering through her, made her blood run hot and heavy.

'Sweet, oh so sweet...' Colby's voice was saturated with pleasure, his fingers trembled as he clutched a handful of her pale hair. 'God, you smell so good...' His lips brushed over her neck, down over her collarbone. 'You taste so good,' he whispered. 'So good...'

'Colby...' Greer's voice was thick, unrecognizable. She felt her mind drifting away, her common sense lost in a dark mist of desire...

But when Colby unbuttoned her blouse, when she felt his hot breath fan the sensitive hollow between her breasts, when she felt his hands slide up her back and touch the clasp of her bra, sanity returned with a jolt.

With a little sound in her throat, she jerked free.

Colby made no move to pull her back into his arms. Breathing raggedly, he leaned against the wall again, one hand dragging slowly over his chest, as if he were trying to steady heartbeats that—like hers—were racing out of control.

Greer's fingers shook as she buttoned her blouse. 'You were right.' Her voice was low. 'I shouldn't have come.'

She didn't look at him as she passed him on her way to the steps. And this time he didn't try to stop her. But when she'd clambered halfway down to the lower level, she thought she heard him call after her.

She must, of course, have imagined it. Colby wanted her, wanted to take her to his bed. He didn't love her, didn't even care for her. And the voice she had heard calling her name had been embued with emotion, an emotion that had sounded painfully like love.

Oh, yes...she knew she must have imagined that. Colby Daken might feel a lot of things for her...but love would never be one of them.

CHAPTER SIX

GREER'S apartment was on the twenty-first floor of a high rise just off Yonge Street, a couple of blocks from St. Clair. When she locked the door behind her early that evening, after the long drive back from the lake, she felt utterly exhausted and thankful to be home...modest though that home was.

The apartment had a small living room with a sweeping view of the city, and a bedroom with space for little more than her bed. Crossing the room, she dropped her handbag on the duvet, placed her weekend bag on the Persian rug and stifling a yawn, crossed to the adjoining bathroom.

After a shower, she put on a shortie robe and made for the kitchen. There she poured a generous glass of chilled white wine before meandering through to the sitting room. Her ceiling-high bookcase was crammed with books, and with recent editions of *Women's Wear Daily, Vogue, Town and Country*... and sitting atop a pile of gourmet cookbooks was her answering machine. The red light was blinking. Greer pressed Play, and sinking into the squashy cushions of her gray futon with her bare feet curled under her, she listened to her messages.

Call me when you get back! That was her best friend Gillian, a sales assistant with a Bay Street stockbroking firm. *Rick's going back to his wife—can you believe that jerk? After all he's put me through...*

Greer chuckled as she listened to the dismal wail.

The second message was from Tony, an old school friend who lived in Parry Sound. *Coming to TO next week—hope we can do lunch. Will phone again Tuesday...*

Greer sipped her wine as she listened to the remaining messages...six in all...from friends who just wanted to touch base. As usual, there was nothing to upset her, provoke her, disturb her. She kept her personal life on an even keel...and that was simple to do; she chose her friends carefully...especially her male friends...and she avoided falling in love. She was aware that in playing safe, she was probably missing out on some great highs...but she was also protecting herself from some agonizing lows. On balance, she was sure she'd made the right decision.

But now Colby had come back into her life and in the course of one short weekend, was threatening to destroy her carefully built-up equilibrium. It scared her half to death, and even thinking about him set her body shivering.

Swallowing the last of her wine in an almost panicky gulp, she put down her glass and pushed herself to her feet. She would call Gillian, and listen as her redheaded friend melodramatically poured out all her woes; and then, she knew, they'd laugh, because when they talked, invariably Gillian would start to see the funny side of whatever situation she'd landed herself in, and would make some pithy self-derisive comment that would make them both crack up.

With a wry smile, Greer punched in Gillian's number. Thank heavens, she thought, for friends.

When Greer arrived at work on Monday morning, it was to find her partner and marketing manager, Bill Pine, pacing the floor by her secretary's desk, his bony face taut.

'We have to find another four seamstresses,' he burst out the moment he saw her. 'I've just flown in from Munich and—'

'I gather your trip was successful, then?' Greer cocked
her eyebrow teasingly as he glowered at her. They made
a perfect team; Bill regularly pulled tantrums like the
one he was pulling right now, and she regularly calmed
him down, by making him discuss their problem logi-
cally. Together they invariably came up with a solution
they could both live with. They both thrived on the challenge . . . though she knew Bill would have vehemently
denied such an idea. 'The buyers liked our product?'

Her partner dragged a hand through his shock of
caramel brown hair. 'Where the hell are we going to find
another four *reliable* seamstresses?' He glared at Greer
accusingly, as if this quandary was all her fault . . . which
she supposed it was, since it was the growing popularity
of her designs that was creating this increasingly hungry
market. 'You think it's going to be *easy?*'

'Whoever promised you life was going to be easy!'
Grinning, Greer sailed past him into her office, calling
over her shoulder to her secretary, 'Bill needs his caf-
feine fix, Tina. Can you scrounge up a mug of coffee?'

'Sure—one for you, too?'

'Bless you, Tina!' She held the door open and gestured to Bill to come in. 'Sit down,' she said. 'Let's talk.'

The hectic pace continued all week, with one problem
arising after the other—she and Bill managing, somehow,
to sort them all out between them. Normally, by Friday
afternoon, she was more than ready to call it quits and
go home, but on this particular Friday she found herself
looking for excuses to stay on in her office.

Around five thirty, Tina poked her head around the
door. 'I'm off then.'

Greer was standing by a partially clad mannequin,
painstakingly adjusting folds of purple silk. She looked
up, her expression vague. 'What was that, Tina?'

Tina chuckled. 'You're married to your work, aren't
you! Well, I'm not . . . I'm married to Bob Winslow, and

if I don't get out of here fast, he's going to find some other floozy to take to the movies. How about you—do you have plans for the weekend...or are you going to spend it here with Cindy-baby?'

Greer forced a smile. 'I'm going to the cottage.'

Tina's eyes became dreamy. 'The cottage. Lucky you. Sand and sun and cool water, barbecues, and books, and walks in the woods.' She grinned mischievously. 'Ah well, Brad Pitt's the next best thing. I'm going to spend the evening with him. Too bad Bob's going to be there, too!'

After she left, her footsteps echoing hollowly on the tiled floor of the lobby, Greer stood back from the mannequin, looked at it for a frowning moment and then impatiently flicked off the length of silk and tossed it among the bolts of fabric on a nearby table.

She retrieved her handbag from her desk, and as she made for the door, called back to the now-naked mannequin, 'See you Monday, Cindy-baby. Have a co...ool weekend!'

Darkness was closing in by the time she reached the lake, but as Greer let her Toyota coast down the track, she saw Colby. He was walking up from the beach, his light-colored shirt absorbing the glare of her headlamps. Her heart performed a couple of cartwheels...at least she could give no other explanation for the disturbance she felt behind her rib cage...and her pulse raced forward in a crazy race to nowhere.

Fingers clutched around the steering wheel, Greer dipped her foot on the brake, in preparation for rounding the corner at the foot of the track.

But when she reached the corner, Colby stepped in front of the vehicle, and waved her down.

Cursing beneath her breath, she braked hard and rolled to a halt just feet away from him. He strode around the bonnet and leaning one elbow on the roof of the car, bent to the open window. In the dim light from the dashboard, their eyes met, and when Greer saw the dusky gleam in his, she wondered if he was remembering the passion that had trembled between them at their last meeting.

But when he spoke, his tone gave no sign of any such thoughts on his part. 'Jem's in bed,' he said flatly. 'She was baking all morning—did too much and decided to turn in early. I've been watching out for you, so I could warn you before you went in, in case you called out and wakened her.'

'She's all right, though? Not sick, or anything?'

'No, just tired. She'll be fine by morning.'

He was standing bare inches from the car; Greer could almost feel the heat emanating from his body...she could certainly smell his familiar male scent, and the intimacy of it hurled her into a panic. Snatching her foot off the brake, she said hurriedly, 'Well, thanks for letting me know about Gran. I'll be quiet when I go in...'

'Hang on a minute.' Colby's long-fingered hand curved over the bottom frame of the open window, and once again, Greer braked. 'Have you eaten?' he asked.

'Yes, I stopped for a bite on the way here. Now, if you'll excuse me, I'm tired, I've had a busy week, I just want to put my feet up and—'

'Come in for a nightcap.' A loon's lonely cry drifted over the lake, mingling with the strains of polka music from a far-off accordion. 'There's something I want to ask you.'

'So...ask.'

'Oh, for God's sake, can't you just come in for a drink without making a big deal of it?'

'What's the matter, Colby? Lost your touch? Surely you can't be so hard up for sex that you've had to wait around for little old me? Sorry, I'm not interested. But hey...tell you what I'll do—I'll baby-sit Jamie if you want to drive to the Green Lady Bar up the road—you should have no problem picking up some willing woman there—'

'Did I say anything about sex?' Colby's voice was quiet. 'As far as I recall, all I offered you was a drink. Perhaps you're the one who's losing your touch, Greer.'

Greer closed her eyes. She rubbed her nape. She exhaled a weary breath. 'Sorry,' she muttered. 'Forget I said that. I really am bushed, but I'll come in if it's something important.' She reached out to switch off the ignition, but before she could, Colby said,

'Leave it running. I apologize, too—of course you're tired . . . I should have taken that into consideration. I won't keep you a minute. What I want to say is this. I've been in touch with an agency in Toronto and have set up some nanny interviews midweek. I'll be taking Jamie to town with me and when I've seen all the likely prospects, and narrowed my list to two, I'll have him meet them later on in the day. I was wondering if you'd be free Wednesday to look after him while I do the preliminary interviewing.'

Shock blasted through Greer, leaving her limp. She slumped back in her seat. So Colby had decided to move back for good, otherwise he wouldn't be hiring a nanny here. What on earth was she going to do about the cottage? Oh, dammit, she wailed silently, the cottage was the *least* of her worries. The sixty-four-thousand-dollar question was: What was she going to do about her *life?* How was she going to bear it, knowing Colby was living in Toronto, knowing she might bump into him at any minute—

'Greer? Could you help me out on this?'

With an effort, Greer gathered herself together. 'So . . . does this mean you're moving back here?'

'Yes.'

'And you're going to go through with your plan?' She injected icy disapproval into her tone. 'Once you've hired a nanny, you're going to hire a *mistress?*'

Colby had stepped back, and now the moon was bright on his face, its white light harshly revealing the expression in his eyes, an expression of pain and frustration. 'You think you can come up with some better idea?' He sounded intensely weary, as if he'd already turned the problem over and over in his own mind, to the point of exhaustion.

'I think Jamie deserves a mother. A proper mother. And a proper family. The arrangement you've decided to set up—' Greer shook her head '—it's cold, cut-and-dried. Without heart. Not the best way to bring up a child—'

'I gather then, since you're opposed to my hiring a nanny, that you'll be unavailable to baby-sit Jamie?'

'No, I'll make myself available.' And it's not the nanny part I've a problem with, she wanted to cry, it's the other... the mistress part. 'It'll be a pleasure to spend time with Jamie. When may I expect you?'

'We'll drive up on Tuesday night, stay at the Harbour Castle. My first interview is scheduled for nine, at the agency office on Yonge Street.'

'Then drop Jamie at my apartment. Around eight? I'll give you my address before I leave here.'

'Thanks. I appreciate it.' He took another step back. 'Good night, then.'

'Good night,' she said, and releasing the brake, swung the car around the corner, and drove it with as little sound as possible up the driveway to the parking space by the Westbury cottage. She sat there for some time, lost in her tumbled thoughts, before finally getting out and crossing quietly to the side door. She had just opened it, and was about to pull it gently shut, when she heard a cry.

She froze. Had the sound come from farther away, she might have mistaken it for the call of a loon, but it came from close by. It came from Colby's cottage...and it was the cry of a child.

As it came again, she felt her blood chill. It was the wail of a little boy waking from a nightmare. Every motherly instinct in her urged her to run toward the cry, urged her to offer comfort to the unhappy child.

But it wasn't her responsibility. It was Colby's.

And she would have to let him handle it alone.

Tomorrow, though, she would make a special effort to spend time with Jamie; he needed a woman's touch...not the touch of a nanny, as Colby had decided; and certainly not the touch of some female hired to give Colby sex and nothing more.

Jamie needed tenderness and reassurance from people who loved him. She, and his grandmother, could offer him that.

'Jamie was crying last night, Gran.'

'Was he, dear? Oh, I'm so sorry.' Jem was sitting up in bed, her hands around the mug of strong sweet tea Greer had just brought her. 'That poor child.'

Greer crossed to the bedroom window, and looked out. It was only eight, but already a haze was shimmering up off the lake. She could see the Pierson children, playing by the water's edge, could see Brad out on the float; Lisa would be cooking breakfast...

Would Colby be cooking breakfast next door, for Jamie? How had he coped last night? she wondered. Should she have followed her instincts and gone knocking at his door? She sighed heavily; sometimes it was so hard to know what was the right thing to do.

'You sound as if you have all the cares of the world on your shoulders this morning!' Jem said. 'That was a heavy sigh, if ever I heard one! Did you have a busy week?'

Greer turned. 'Hectic, Gran—but that wasn't the reason for my sigh. I was just wondering if I should have offered some help when I heard Jamie last night. Perhaps Colby's finding it hard to deal with his son. After all, it's only six months since Eleanor died—he has his own grief to cope with...'

'Colby's a grown man and he'll have to find his own salvation, but the boy.' Jem uttered a vexed exclamation. 'That's a different matter. I'm afraid I didn't see much of him this week—I just didn't feel myself. Oh, I told Colby and the others I'd spent too much time in the kitchen, but it was more than that—I'd had a stomach bug working on me for days. At any rate, I'm over it now. I feel a hundred-percent this morning...well, perhaps ninety-eight percent,' she amended with a wry smile. 'If we both try to spend time with the child, I'm sure that'll help. Colby needn't know what we're doing. We don't want him to feel...inadequate.'

The thought of Colby Daken feeling inadequate in any way was laughable...yet in this one area of his life, he was perhaps out of his depth. And Jem, Greer thought with a frown, still looked a bit peaky. So it would be up to her, Greer, to try to help Jamie...at least, today. But do it without Colby's noticing? That might be difficult.

Still, she would try.

'Greer, Colby told me he's going to sell his Melbourne business and start over in Toronto. Isn't it wonderful? And he's so kind—he said that if you don't want the cottage, I ought to keep it on, at least for a few more years. He's offered to drive me up here anytime he makes the trip with Jamie. It's like an answer to a prayer.'

'Isn't it, Gran!' Greer somehow managed a smile. 'Now...would you like some more toast?'

'No, dear, but I think I'll stay in bed awhile—have a little snooze...keep my strength for the surprise party tonight. You hadn't forgotten about it, had you?'

'No, I hadn't forgotten.'

'Good.' Jem put the mug on her bedside table and sank back happily on her pillows. 'What are you going to do now?'

'I'm going to tidy the kitchen, catch up on the washing and then go for a swim. And after that—' Greer looped a strand of blond hair behind her ear '—I shall look for Jamie, and see if I can get him to open up a little.'

She was leaving the cottage, wearing her white one-piece swimsuit, a scarlet beach towel slung around her shoulders, when she heard a low *'Psst!'*

Turning curiously toward the sound, she saw Brad at the side of the path, lurking behind the trunk of a birch tree. He signaled to her to come over.

'Greer,' he whispered, 'your grandmother wasn't around last night so I couldn't get the party food transferred from my cooler to her fridge. I waited around for you...but I didn't hear you arrive. Were you late coming in?'

'Not that late...but Colby warned me that Gran wasn't feeling well and had gone to bed, so I didn't make a noise, or put on any lights...'

'Is Jem okay now?'

'Fine. She's looking forward to the party.'

'Great. Look, I have the cooler here.' Greer noticed that a large red cooler was standing at the foot of the tree. 'And I'd like to sneak it into your kitchen now, while Lisa's busy cooking breakfast.'

'Come on in.'

Greer led the way inside, and it took just a few minutes to get the food unloaded and into Jem's large fridge. When they'd finished, Greer suggested Brad store the cooler in the walk-in cupboard, just in case Lisa spotted him bringing it back to their place.

'Good thinking.' Brad stuffed the cooler where she suggested, behind a case of apple juice. 'You'd make a great criminal, Greer—covering all bases!'

They chuckled, and were still chuckling as they walked down the steps outside. When they reached the birch tree where they'd met up, Brad made to leave, but he'd just gone past the tree when Greer stepped off the path after him.

'Brad,' she whispered, and he turned, 'Gran says she's fine...but what if she's not up to getting Lisa out of the way before dinner as arranged—how are you and I going to manage to get everything set up for the surprise!'

Brad leaned one hand against the tree trunk and looked down at Greer. 'Now there's a snag I hadn't considered.'

'Oh, don't worry—we'll find *some* way to get rid of everybody, even if it means telling a few white lies...'

'Lisa would be amazed if she knew about all this subterfuge—'

'Going on under her pretty little nose! Ah well.' Greer touched his arm affectionately as she looked up at him with a warm smile. 'It's all in the name of love!'

The sound of footsteps on the path was the first intimation they weren't alone. Turning sharply, hoping whoever it was hadn't heard anything that would give away any inkling of the surprise party, Greer felt her heart slam against her breastbone when she saw the intruder was Colby.

His grim expression struck her with foreboding.

'Well, well, well,' he said, his voice deceptively calm, 'what have we here?'

Oh, Lord...what rotten timing! But before either she or Brad could answer, Lisa's voice came drifting from the direction of the Pierson cottage: 'Brad Pierson, where are you? If you know what's good for you, you'll get in here right this instant before your bacon and eggs congeal!' A howl of children's laughter followed this dire warning.

'Good morning, Colby.' Brad threw Greer a questioning glance; she shook her head almost imperceptibly, intimating that she'd be okay. His features relaxed. 'I'd love to stay and shoot the breeze but hell hath no fury, as they say!'

He strode away, leaving Greer to face Colby alone.
And if the look in Colby's eyes was anything to go by,
at this moment the man considered her, in the hierarchy
of life, to be lower than the lowest snail.

'Good morning!' she said airily. Over his swim shorts
he was wearing an unbuttoned shirt of icy blue, and the
cold color was reflected in his eyes, making the irises as
clear as glass... glass that was like a windowpane revealing his anger. 'Excuse me... I'm going for a dip.'

She walked away with brisk steps, but was immediately aware that she wasn't going to get free of him that
easily; with a few swift strides he caught up with her,
and strode alongside her as she made for the water.

'How's Jem?' he asked brusquely.

'Much better. She's resting up for tonight's... she's
resting up for tonight. We're going out for dinner.' Greer
looked around pointedly toward the Trillium Lodge,
hoping Colby would infer that was where they were going
to eat.

There was no more conversation as they walked, but
the tension between them escalated with every step, and
Greer braced herself for what was to come. Once at the
water's edge, she grasped the ends of her scarlet towel
and whirling around, glared up at him. 'You're obviously following me for a purpose. Do you want to tell
me what that purpose is?'

'You know damned well what it is.' His voice was
gravelly. 'How many times do I have to warn you to
keep away from Brad Pierson! Haven't you done *enough*
damage? Didn't you learn your lesson eight years ago,
when your behavior was no better than that of a common
slut—'

Greer almost doubled over, his attack affecting her as
physically as a punch in the stomach. Fighting a sudden
surge of nausea, she stared up at him defiantly.

'Who appointed you my keeper?' she snapped. 'What
I do is none of your business—'

'I'm making it my business! Lisa's an old friend of mine and I'm not going to let you—'

'You can't control me, Colby Daken! And it would suit you better to spend your time with your son, instead of spying on me, like some perverted Peeping Tom! Jamie *needs* you, you big oaf...whereas I *certainly* don't!'

She knew by the sudden pallor of his face that she'd struck gold with her remark about Jamie. Ignoring a stab of remorse, she spun away, the movement setting her blond hair swinging, and flinging her towel down on the sand, she ran along the water's edge, fast, and out onto the wooden jetty.

When she was halfway along, she plunged into the water in a running dive, gasping for breath as her sun-warmed body hit the cool surface.

Colby Daken was blind, she reflected bitterly as she swam with powerful strokes to the float; and he was a fool; and he had hurt her more than he could ever know.

Why, then, considering all this, was she still so hopelessly and irrevocably in love with him!

CHAPTER SEVEN

BRAD took the four children fishing that morning, and after they came back, Colby whisked his son away in his Jeep. The two were away all afternoon, so Greer's plans to have a chat with Jamie had to be put on hold, but she promised herself she'd make an opportunity to talk with him that evening.

Brad had scheduled the party for six o'clock, and at five, Greer found herself in the Westbury kitchen, blowing up balloons. She was just about to start puffing up a long blue one when Jem opened the screen door from outside. Without coming in, she said softly,

'Did you tell Colby you and I were going to the Trillium Lodge for our evening meal?'

'I didn't actually *say* that...but I certainly tried to give him that impression.'

'You convinced him! And Brad told Lisa he's going to take the family into Parry Sound for dinner—he's invited Colby and Jamie to join them—but he told them he wants to have a snooze first and suggested we all go for a walk so he can have some peace!' Winking, she called in a loud voice that would be sure to carry, 'Greer, darling, I'm going for a stroll with Lisa and Colby—I'll be back in an hour or so!' She threw Greer a conspiratorial smile. 'How's that for good acting?' she whispered.

'Bette Davis, move over!' Greer made a shooing motion with one hand. 'Off you go—Brad and I have tons of stuff to do. Can you *really* keep everybody away for an hour?'

Jem gestured with her cane. 'Leave it to Bette!'

*   *   *

Greer arranged Brad's artistically assembled shish kebabs on the white hot coals of the barbecue and as the lamb and vegetable chunks began to spit and sizzle, she stepped back and looked at them admiringly.

'Very neat and perfectly color coordinated, Brad! You're quite the expert!'

He grinned. 'It's Lisa's all-time dinner favorite, so I've had plenty of practice.' He cocked an eyebrow. 'I've worked up a nice thirst—how about you? Fancy a drink?'

'Sounds good.'

'Beer or wine?'

'Beer, I think. Might cool me down a bit!'

'Beer it is. Be right back.'

Brad went inside, and Greer took the opportunity to nip down the veranda steps and peek along the beach to check where the others were. She saw them in the distance. Colby and Jamie were walking together—together yet apart; the Pierson children were splashing around at the water's edge; and Jem, she noticed with satisfaction, was trailing behind with Lisa. Those two would arrive last, and that would give Brad time to let the others in on the secret, before Jem led the unsuspecting birthday girl up to the veranda.

'They'll be a few minutes yet,' she said to Brad as she returned to the deck and found him there. 'I just checked.'

'Good,' he said. 'Your beer, milady. I must say you deserve it, after all that hard work.'

'I do!' Greer smiled ruefully. 'One more balloon and my cheeks would have burst wide open.'

Brad held up his mug. 'Cheers.'

'Good health.' Greer took a hearty swallow, savoring the cold beer's full-bodied tang as much as its thirst-quenching quality. 'So...what are you and the kids giving Lisa for her birthday?'

'They've clubbed together and bought her a Walkman.'

'And you?'

'I've splurged on a bottle of her favorite perfume. Coco.'

'Lisa likes silk lingerie, so Jem and I are giving her one of my latest creations.' Greer smiled teasingly. 'I think you're going to appreciate it as much as Lisa.'

'I am, am I?' Brad grinned. 'What is it? Something in black and scarlet, designed to drive a man crazy?'

Greer waved an admonitory finger. 'Patience, patience. Half the fun is in the anticipation. Don't they say that to travel hopefully is a better thing than to arrive?'

'Oh, I can't say I'd agree on that score.' Brad's voice was threaded with amusement. 'The arriving can be pretty exciting, too!'

'Bradley Pierson, you're talking to a single lady— watch your tongue!'

Brad guffawed, but even as Greer started to laugh, too, a sound at the far end of the deck caught her attention. When Colby appeared at the top of the shallow flight of steps, her heart jumped, then skipped a couple of beats.

Sweat glistened on his brow, and his face was flushed, as if he'd been running. Had he jogged ahead of the others? He must have done, otherwise he couldn't possibly have been here already. At any rate, his expression was thunderous. Had he seen her when she'd popped down to the beach below the Pierson cottage a few moments ago? Had he realized she must be with Brad? Oh, Lord...

'Colby!' Her voice shook a little. 'You're back.'

Brad, still chuckling and obviously not sensing Colby's ominous mood, said, 'Hey, come and have a beer—'

Colby ignored Brad, and strode menacingly toward Greer. She slid her beer mug onto the railing and took a step back.

'Colby.' Her pulse fluttered apprehensively. 'Brad and
I were—'

She gasped as Colby grabbed her by the shoulders and
turned her toward the steps. 'Get the hell out of here,'
he ordered harshly, 'before Lisa gets back. My God, I
can't believe your gall—the minute Jem's back is turned,
the minute Lisa's out of sight, you're in here like Flynn—
and Pierson—' his tone was blistering '—saying he
wanted to have a snooze—'

But Brad had apparently—finally—twigged what was
going on and outrage blazed in his expression.

'You're out of your mind, Colby! Good grief—it's
Lisa's birthday... Greer and I have organized a surprise
party—get a grip on yourself!'

He shoved Colby backward, the attack abrupt. Caught
by surprise, Colby released his grip on Greer, but she,
too, was taken unawares, and she lost her balance and
fell forward against Colby's chest.

Automatically he put his arms around her to catch
her, and for a fraction of a second she was aware of
nothing but the disturbing male scent of his body, the
firm pressure of his hands on her back, his minty breath
fanning her face...

She felt her legs wobble. Even in a situation like this,
she found the man irresistible. With bitter anger welling
inside her—anger directed at herself as much as at
Colby—she wrenched herself free.

'Colby Daken.' She glared at him. 'You're a prize ass!
What's the matter with you? Why do you always think
the *worst* of people? Look around and you'll see *exactly*
what Brad and I have been doing!'

Features still twisted with emotion, Colby looked
around and Greer thought she heard a swift intake of
breath as he took in the blue and green balloons, the
birthday streamers, the sizzling shish kebabs, the gaily
wrapped parcels, the table set prettily with multicolored
napkins and glasses. And she knew, by the flicker of his

eyelids, the flexing of a muscle in his jaw, that he realized he'd been mistaken. She almost felt sorry for him. *Almost.*

He cleared his throat as he turned to Brad.

'Sorry, Pierson.' His tone was strained. 'It seems that...*this* time...I was out of line.'

'Not seems. You *were.*' Brad's voice was tight with anger. 'But don't waste your time apologizing to me— I can take anything you care to dish out. Apologize to Greer.'

'Forget it, Brad, it doesn't matter,' Greer said wearily, and added, as she heard the sound of approaching voices, 'All right if I go inside and freshen up?'

'Go ahead, honey.'

In the bathroom, Greer took one look at her stark reflection in the mirror, and with a grimace, started splashing icy cold water onto her face.

When she walked back across the sitting room a couple of minutes later, she could see through the patio doors that everyone except Jem and Lisa was now assembled on the deck. Brad had obviously let the children in on the secret, and their faces were glowing with excitement; even Jamie's face quivered in a tentative smile.

Colby was standing by the patio door, and she could see his profile etched against the sky. He had a magnificent profile...just looking at it made her feel all mushy—

Boor! Jerk! Nincompoop! He was all of those things and more. She put out her hand to sweep open the door, but he must have been waiting for her and sensed the movement. He jumped into action. Flicking the screen back, he said, in a low, husky voice, 'Greer, I—'

Head high, she stalked past him and crossed to the other side of the deck. If he wanted to apologize, it was too late. The man was *obsessed* with what he believed was a liaison between her and Brad. Even if it had been true, it would have been absolutely none of his business.

She snuck a quick look at him...and saw that his gaze was fixed on her, his eyes dark and smolderingly intense.

She tilted her chin and turned slightly, so that her shoulder was to him. The cold shoulder. She hoped he was able to interpret the significance of the gesture.

'...I've enjoyed our walk, Lisa.' Jem's words preceded her up the steps. 'And yes, I'd love to have a glass of sherry with you, before we all set out for dinner.'

On reaching the deck, Jem flashed Brad a smug thumbs-up sign before tapping her way across to stand by Greer.

A second later, Lisa appeared. She was running a casual hand over her brown hair as she got to the top of the steps, but when she saw the assembled crowd—family and friends—all facing her way with beaming smiles, she froze.

'*Guys?* What on earth's going—'

She got no further. Eight voices, as one, interrupted her, and their shout of '*Surprise!*' was echoed by their own whoops of glee, because it was obvious from Lisa's shriek of delight that the party was indeed a total surprise to her.

Greer thought she would have to spend the next few hours trying to avoid Colby, but not so. If anything, he went out of his way to avoid her, and after a while, she felt her tension ease a little and she began to enjoy herself.

The party was a great success, and Lisa was showered with gifts. Even Colby came up with something—he slipped away to his cottage and brought back a bottle of Duty Free Drambuie he'd bought en route from Australia. Lisa was thrilled with her Walkman and her perfume...and with her *Passing Fancy* creation...though Brad gave a groan of mock-disappointment when it turned out to be no erotic fantasy in black and scarlet lace but an elegant white silk robe.

Around eight o'clock, after dishes had been done and the adults were sitting around chatting over coffee, Greer noticed that though the Pierson children were playing leapfrog down on the lawn, Jamie wasn't with them.

Excusing herself, she went in search of him, and found him sitting cross-legged...and alone...on the beach, below the Daken cottage.

'Fancy a walk?' Casually she slipped her hands into the pockets of her culottes as she looked down at him.

He didn't look up. 'No, thanks.'

'Too bad. I could sure use the company. I missed out on the walk you all had earlier, because I was helping Mr. Pierson get the party ready.' She paused, and then said, in a coaxing tone, 'Sure I can't make you change your mind?'

He shook his head. Greer hesitated, then she sat down on the sand beside him. He lifted his head then, but not to look at her; he stared out at a speedboat that was skimming across the middle of the lake.

'Noisy things, those speedboats,' Greer murmured. 'I much prefer rowboats, like the *Summer Sprite.*' She looped her hands around her bent knees. 'You know, when I came to the lake the first time, I was the same age as you are now. Seven. And like you—' Greer lifted a handful of sand and let it dribble through her fingers '—I'd just lost my mom. My dad, too, actually.'

Jamie didn't say anything. He just stared out over the water. His profile was to her, so she couldn't see the expression in his eyes. She took a deep breath and looked down at her sandals. She had no experience with children, and felt herself floundering.

'Mom and Dad had a hardware store in Calgary. They ran the business together and rarely managed to get away on holiday, but when they won a skiing trip in British Columbia, they made arrangements to have me stay over at a friend's house, and paid someone to come in and look after the store. On the last day of their holiday, they got caught in an avalanche and died. Your great-grandmother has looked after me ever since.

'When she brought me to the cottage that first summer, I was such a sad little girl.' Greer felt her eyes prick; just talking about that time reminded her of the aching loneliness she'd suffered.

Blinking back the tears, she glanced at Jamie.

He was still looking out over the lake, and judging by his grim scowl, she hadn't gotten through to him. What had she expected, she wondered, as she succumbed to a feeling of helplessness? If his own father couldn't connect with him, what had made her so presumptuous as to think she could! All she had done was intrude on his privacy—butt in where she obviously wasn't wanted.

With a sigh, she unlooped her arms. She ought to apologize. But even as she decided to do just that, Jamie scrambled to his feet and made to take off.

She leaned over and caught his hand. 'Jamie, I'm sorry if—'

His head jerked around and when she saw his face, her heart gave an agonizing twist. Oh, she had gotten through to him all right, and far more successfully than she'd ever dared hope. Behind his glasses, Jamie's eyes were swimming in tears; and his features had crumpled—contorted with effort and pain—as he tried desperately not to break down.

'Come here.' She tugged his arm gently, and he tumbled down beside her. She took his hand, and held it tightly. 'It'll get better.' Her voice was husky. 'It really will, Jamie. I promise you. After a while, it will get better.'

He started to sob, and she put her arm around him, drew him close. After a long while, the sobbing subsided, and in the end, with a last hiccuping gulp, he took off his glasses, and wiped his fingertips over his eyes.

'Your daddy was killed, too?' His voice was wobbly.

She nodded. 'That's right.'

He put on his glasses again, and looked directly into Greer's face. For a long moment he scanned it, as if searching for something. In the end, he said, in a little whisper, 'You *are* pretty. Fact, you have the prettiest eyes I've ever seen.'

Oh, Lord...Greer felt as if her heart was breaking. 'You're not too bad-looking yourself,' she said in a teasing tone that she hoped would bring Jamie's tension down to a more bearable level. 'In fact, if you were twenty years older, I might just fancy you!' Which was, of course, the unhappy truth. In twenty years, the son would be a clone of the father, and Colby *was* her fancy. Had always been her fancy. She jumped to her feet, and pulled Jamie up beside her. 'I think,' she said, 'we're ready for that walk now. Okay?'

Jamie pushed up his glasses, and gave a wavering smile as he dusted the beach sand from his swim shorts. 'Okay.'

'Better tell your dad where you're going, in case he comes looking for you.'

Greer watched as Jamie made for the steps leading up to the Piersons' veranda. She'd made a breakthrough, and she was profoundly thankful for that. But would that breakthrough extend to the relationship between Colby and his son? Only time would tell, but she prayed it would be so.

Jamie came back alone, which, of course, was exactly what Greer had expected. There had been no chance Colby would invite himself along. Perhaps he'd initially thought he should apologize for his accusatory behavior before the party, but his attitude during the event had clearly shown he had rethought his position.

And that was just fine with her. The last thing she wanted to do was spend time with him. Then why was it that when Jamie had come back on his own, she'd felt something suspiciously like disappointment?

Jamie squinted up at her. 'Dad says it'll soon cool off and I'm to go in and get a shirt.'

'Good idea. And better get something on your feet.'

Jamie took off toward the Daken cottage and came back a minute or two later, feet in sneakers, arms struggling up into the sleeves of a white sweatshirt.

'Here,' Greer offered, 'let me help you with that. You've got the sleeves inside out.'

'Can we go along the trail?' Jamie asked. 'Sarah says there's always lots of squirrels playing under the trees.'

'Sure.'

As they walked along the beach toward the trail, a companionable silence settled between them. Jamie had obviously recovered from his bout of weeping, and seemed more cheerful than Greer had ever seen him.

When they reached the entrance to the trail, they passed Colby's Jeep, which was parked in his carport. In the driveway, was a pile of lumber.

'Your dad's going to be working on the boathouse, isn't he?' Greer said.

'Some bits of the walls are rotten. He's going to cut those bits out, and make new ones. He says I can help him. He says he's going to take me fishing. He says we're going to Toronto on Wednesday, and you're going to look after me in the morning. What are we going to do?'

'What would you like to do? We could go to the zoo.'

'Mommy doesn't...didn't like zoos. She said they were smelly and dirty—oh, look.' Jamie's voice was high with excitement. 'A squirrel!'

The squirrel, startled by the noise, scampered away among the trees, and Jamie started after him. Greer's 'Look out for that root' came too late, and the toe of his runner caught under it and he shot forward, to land on his stomach on a bed of damp moss.

'Okay?' Greer helped him to his feet and scooped up his glasses, which had fallen off. He slipped them on again.

'Thanks. I'm fine,' he said. 'But I'm afraid the squirrel's gone.' He glanced down and Greer heard him suck in his breath. 'I've dirtied my shirt—look, it's got green stains on it.' His lips trembled. 'Mommy said—'

'Jamie.' Greer crouched down and put her arms firmly around his thin body. 'You *mustn't* upset yourself if you dirty your clothes... or your knees, or your hands. My goodness, what do you think soap is for!' She gave him a teasing little shake. 'And how do you think the rest of us are going to feel, when we're having fun and getting all grubby, if you just sit there all spanking clean, like some new toy sitting in a box!'

She took in a deep breath. 'Watch this.' Crouching, she ran her right hand, palm down, hard, over the moss... and then over a patch of damp earth for good measure. She lifted her hand to show him the dirt on her skin. 'And watch this.' Deliberately she ran her palm over the shoulder of her blouse, hearing him gasp as the cream silk became soiled. 'Here.' She took his hand, and placed it on the moss. 'Your turn.'

She held her breath for what seemed like forever, and then Jamie—hesitantly, and with the tip of his tongue peeking out—drew his hand over the moss... and, after a long pause, over the damp earth.

He looked up at her, and in his eyes, she saw a spark of adventure. He lifted his hand, but when she realized he'd misunderstood her, and thought she'd invited him to add to the streaks on *her* blouse, she shook her head.

'No, Jamie. Your own shirt.'

His eyes widened. And then she saw the corners of his mouth twitch in a smile. Straightening his shoulders, he drew his palm over the front of his shirt. 'There.' There was a trace of pride in his voice that caught at her heart.

'That wasn't so hard, was it?' Greer said. 'Mind you, I don't recommend you dirty yourself on purpose again. That was just a lesson, to show you that it's okay to get grubby.'

'And I won't get in trouble? Really?'

'No, you won't. I promise.'

'Then—' he chewed his lip, a tentative expression in his eyes '—can we have... a moss fight?'

'A... *moss* fight?'

'Mmm, you know—throwing moss at each other. Sarah told me they do it all the time... they get it in their hair and down their necks and—'

Greer scooped up a bit of moss and tossed it at him.

He let out a startled squeal, but immediately after, with a gleeful chuckle, tugged out a small clump of moss and threw it at Greer. With a giggle, she ducked and it missed her. Jamie snatched up another clump and Greer whirled away with a shriek of mock-alarm, meaning to run back along the path... but instead she bumped into a solid object...

A wide male chest.

She gasped, steadied herself by clutching at the blue shirt in front of her and looked up...

To find herself staring right into Colby's eyes.

He had curved his hands around her waist as he caught her, his fingertips almost reaching the base of her spine, the pads of his thumbs touching a sensitive area just below her ribs. He was holding her so close that when a gust of wind blew a strand of her hair forward, it brushed against his mouth... and stayed there. He lifted one hand and with his long fingers drew the golden filaments from his lips; slowly, as if savoring an indescribably erotic sensation. Once again that hot lashing whip coiled and snapped way down inside Greer, flaming her senses to wild and hungry life.

'Colby.' Her voice was faint. 'What are you doing here? What do you want?'

'What do you think I want?' he said huskily, his gaze drifting to her mouth, lingering there.

'I don't know...'

'I want to apologize.'

Greer looked into his blue eyes and became drowned in a sea of longing, of wanting. 'Apology accepted.'

He cupped the back of her head in one hand, and legs suddenly weak, she felt herself sway toward him, but as he began lowering his head, his intent obvious, she heard Jamie say 'Aunt Greer?' and his voice snapped her back to reality. With a swiftly indrawn breath, she disentangled herself from Colby and turned to look down at Jamie.

His eyes were wary. 'Will you tell Dad about . . . the dirt and stuff. That it's okay now?'

Greer noticed that Colby's breathing was as uneven as her own, but it was the only sign that their near-kiss had affected him in any way. He looked down at Jamie, raised a surprised eyebrow and flicked a finger over the streaks on his son's shirt.

'What have we here?'

'It's dirt,' Greer said. 'I thought it was time Jamie learned it's not the end of the world if he gets grubby.'

'We were having a moss fight, Dad!' Jamie's giggle erupted spontaneously. 'I was *winning*.'

'A moss fight! Now if you'd told me you were planning a moss fight, I would have joined in. But since you kept it a secret.' Colby screwed up his face in a mock-scowl. 'I think I'm going to have to throw you in the lake—shirt and all—and get you cleaned off!'

'You'll have to catch me first!' Jamie yelled. He scooted off down the path, back the way they'd come, looking over his shoulder with a challenging grin every few seconds.

'That's the first time,' Colby said in a stunned voice, 'that I've seen him laugh since . . . Eleanor died. How did you do it, Greer?'

Greer clasped her arms around her waist. 'We talked. I told him I was his age when I first came here, after my parents died. It somehow touched a chord with him and he opened up—'

'Hey, Dad! Come on!'

Greer felt her eyes sting. 'Go,' she said huskily. 'Jamie needs you.'

Colby hesitated for only a fraction of a second, and then he snatched one of Greer's hands.

'If I throw him into the lake—' he swept her along with him as he started back along the trail '—you're going to have to get thrown in, too, because it's all too obvious you were the ringleader here.'

'Oh, Colby...no!' Greer tried unsuccessfully to stifle a giggle. It wouldn't be the first time Colby had thrown her in the lake...but she'd been a teenager then. She was a grown woman now...it wouldn't be...ladylike!

When they reached the beach, Jamie was speeding along the water's edge, screeching in delighted anticipation. In no time at all, Colby had caught him and the child's shouts when his father threw him into the water echoed over the lake and back from the trees...but they were nothing to the exuberant shrieks he emitted a minute or two later as he watched Colby catch Greer and throw her in, too.

When she came up for air, spluttering and totally bedraggled, it was to see father and son, standing on the sand, looking at each other and laughing.

And as she splashed toward them, she put on a great show of outrage, but what she really felt, in her heart, was a wonderful and glowing satisfaction. If she achieved nothing else this summer, she at least had the comfort of knowing that if Colby and Jamie had finally begun to communicate, she had played a part in that minor miracle.

After a hasty shower, Greer changed into jeans and a pink shirt, and returned to the party. Jamie and Colby hadn't come back yet, and for the next while she found herself waiting for them—waiting, tensely, for *Colby*.

After the incident on the beach, Jamie had sprinted off to get changed, and she and Colby had walked up the sand together. They hadn't said much, hadn't even glanced at each other as they walked...but something—something that had made her feel dizzy—had danced invisibly in the air between them...

Something old, something new.

The words echoed in her head as she tried to pin down the ingredients that had subtly tilted their relationship. There was, undoubtedly, harmony, but that had existed before; it was old—it had bloomed between them when she was a child, and she embraced that harmony in the way she would have embraced a threadbare teddy bear from childhood days. It was familiar, and it was comfortable. But the new? Oh, that was far from familiar, far from comfortable. It shivered its way to her nerve endings and excited her almost unbearably. It made her feel restless, and vulnerable...and afraid. But despite that fear, she felt excitement coiling through her like a dark whirlpool.

She was standing leaning against the railing, chatting with Brad and Lisa, when she heard his heavy tread on the steps leading up to the patio. Her back was to the steps, and she fought an almost irresistible urge to whirl around and look at him.

'Where's Jamie?' she heard Sarah ask.

Brad and Lisa turned toward Colby, and... lazily...Greer turned, too. He was smiling—that killer smile that destroyed any hope she had of resisting him— but the smile was directed at Sarah.

'All the excitement of the party caught up with him,' Colby said. 'He dried himself off and then he seemed to be taking forever to get dressed again—when I went through to his room to see what the holdup was, I found him lying on top of his bed...out like a light.'

Jem put up a dainty hand to cover a yawn. 'And bed is where I think I ought to be, too.' She got up. 'Will you all excuse me? And thank you, Lisa, for a lovely party.'

'Don't thank me,' Lisa said. 'Thank Brad and Greer. They did all the work!'

'We did, didn't we!' Brad threw an arm around Greer's shoulders and grinned down at her. 'We make quite a team.'

At that moment, Greer happened to look at Colby, and saw that his gaze was fixed on Brad's arm, his eyes narrowed so she couldn't see their expression ... but she could tell, by the grim compression of his lips, that he was *not* pleased.

The excited anticipation she'd felt just moments ago drained away, leaving in its place an intense weariness. So... Colby had certainly apologized, both to herself and to Brad, but it was obvious he still believed *something* was going on between them.

The knowledge created a tearing pain in her heart.

'Come along, Gran,' she said. 'I'll walk you back. Lisa.' She threw Lisa a warm smile. 'I'm so glad you enjoyed your surprise. It was a lovely party.'

'You're off then?' Lisa sounded surprised.

'Mmm. But I'll see you tomorrow.'

She and Jem had to pass Colby to get off the deck, and as they came alongside him, Greer deliberately averted her eyes and focused her attention on her grandmother.

'Watch that top step, Gran,' she murmured. 'Some sand there ... might be slippery.'

'Good night, Greer.'

Greer felt every muscle in her body tighten as Colby's voice came to her from just inches away.

'Good night,' she said coolly.

'Good night, Colby.' Jem's tone was affectionate. 'It's so nice to have you at the cottage again—isn't it, Greer?'

'Oh, isn't it indeed!' Greer said, knowing that the slight curl of her upper lip would be seen by only Colby.

Cupping her grandmother's elbow, she led her down the steps.

'That's a very unhappy man,' Jem said quietly as she and Greer reached the path leading to the Westbury cottage. 'A very unhappy man indeed.'

'I think he made a lot of headway with Jamie this evening, Gran,' Greer said stiffly. 'They had fun together down by the water...Colby said he hadn't seen Jamie laugh like that since...Eleanor died.'

'Yes, I saw the three of you down there.' Jem paused, as she and Greer reached the side door. 'Funny thing,' she said in an absent tone, 'you looked like a family. The way a family ought to be.'

Greer felt her throat muscles tighten till she could hardly bear the ache. 'Colby doesn't even like me, Gran.' She pushed the door open roughly. 'You know that.'

Jem looked up at Greer, her blue eyes suddenly sharp. 'Oh, he likes you. He's always liked you. In fact, I once thought—' She broke off, with a tiny sound of frustration.

'Thought what, Gran?' Greer stood still, her fingers curved around the edge of the door.

Her grandmother's lips twisted in a wistful smile. 'Oh, it was just an old woman's dream...but I thought...if Eleanor hadn't come on the scene...Colby might one day have fallen in love with you.'

What would Gran say, Greer wondered unhappily as she followed her grandmother inside, if she'd told her that she, too, had once dreamed that Colby would fall in love with her? And what a foolish dream that had been. Eleanor was the one who had stolen his heart, and with an ease that had rocked Greer to the core.

'A one-woman man is what I am,' Colby had declared to Greer that summer. 'And Eleanor is the only one for me.'

Now Eleanor was dead, and Colby would never love again. He would never *let* himself love again; he had made that clear. Instead he planned to find a healthy nubile female to fulfil his sexual needs.

Jem was right. Colby was a very unhappy man. Greer could only hope that the path he had chosen would eventually make him happy once again.

CHAPTER EIGHT

GREER managed to avoid Colby next day, till mid-afternoon, just as she was getting ready to leave. She had said her goodbyes to Jem, who was out back with Jamie, and she was in the kitchen when she saw Colby come across the veranda.

'Hi,' he said through the screen door. 'I've come for your address. If you're still willing to baby-sit, that is.'

'Of course.'

She didn't invite him in, but he came in anyway.

She had written her home address on the back of a business card, and had delegated Jem to deliver it later; now she slid the card off the windowsill and gave it to him. 'My building is just off Yonge Street, a block from St. Clair. There's plenty visitor parking.' She scooped up her bag from the table, and extricating her keys, clinked them impatiently, her message obvious to the point of being rude.

'You're off now?' He tucked the card into the hip pocket of his jeans; Lee jeans that were soft and faded to a sweet baby blue, and clung to his powerful thighs as if there was no place on earth they'd rather be...

This kitchen is too small for the two of us, Greer thought frustratedly; why else would her mind be coming up with such off-the-wall notions! 'Yes,' she said stiffly.

He showed no sign of going. 'See you Wednesday, then.'

'Right.' Fingers slippery, she dropped her keys. She bent to pick them up. He bent over, too. He reached them first, and as she straightened, his breath riffled her hair.

She took the keys, and as his fingers brushed hers, sensitive nerves started quivering someplace deep inside her. 'Thanks.' Her voice had an unfamiliar huskiness.

'My pleasure.'

And her pleasure, too. Oh, certainly her pleasure. A tender sweetness flooded through her veins. Colby's gaze was no longer bland. It burned with an electrical intensity that set warning bells shrilling in her soul. This man, she decided as a bead of perspiration trickled down her spine, should be legally compelled to wear a sign saying: Surgeon General's Warning. Looking Into These Eyes Can Be Hazardous To Your Health.

'I'm leaving.' Her tone had more than an edge of panic.

Shoving him aside blindly to get to the door, she took him by surprise and gave him no chance to stop her; but as the door swung shut behind her and she walked quickly across the veranda to the steps, she heard him call after her, 'Leaving... or running?'

His taunting words were still echoing in her head when she was halfway home.

The weather in Toronto was stiflingly close, and by Tuesday night the humidity was so high the entire city wilted. A storm was forecast... and it broke on Wednesday. At the exact moment Greer opened her door to Colby and Jamie, the first flash of lightning zigzagged its blinding path across a sky that since dawn had been as black as ink.

'I'm afraid there'll be no zoo today, Jamie.' Thunder muttered ominously as Greer took the child's light anorak. 'We'll have to think of something else to do.'

'Maybe I can watch TV.' Jamie pushed up his glasses in a gesture Greer was finding increasingly endearing.

'Good morning, Greer.'

She had avoided looking at Colby; now she had no choice. He was, she saw, wearing a crisp white shirt, a striped silk tie and a pair of dark suit pants—a sexy combination on any well-built attractive man, but on Colby it was dynamite.

'Good morning.' Her breath caught in her throat as their eyes met; was she going to see the mocking challenge that had been there last time they met? No, his gaze was casual. For today, at least, there was to be a truce. With a sense of relief, she ushered him into the sitting room. He rounded the glass-and-brass coffee table and crossed to the huge picture window.

'It's going to be quite a storm,' he murmured, 'and you have a grandstand seat. What a fantastic view. Come over here, Jamie—' Jamie joined him and he put an arm around his son's shoulders '—that's the CN Tower to the right...we'll have to go up there sometime...but certainly not today!'

'What's that water behind all those high rises? Is it the sea?' Jamie asked.

'No, that's Lake Ontario. And way over there in back—that's New York State.'

Jamie and his father appeared to be getting along well, and thank heaven for that! Greer reflected, as she hung Jamie's jacket in the hall closet before returning to the sitting room. There was a naturalness between them that had been missing before the moss fight.

'Colby,' she said, 'when will you be back?'

He turned. 'The agency has lined up six possibles. My last interview is at one. Two o'clock okay?'

'Fine.' She was visited by a vivid picture of six Playboy centerfolds strutting around an office, Colby behind a desk, his chair tilted, his feet up, his blue eyes glazed.

'Good.' Those blue eyes flicked over her, and as they lingered on the curves under her yellow cotton top, she felt her head spin. She walked out into the narrow hall, and opened the door.

Colby tousled Jamie's hair. 'Have a good day.'

'You too, Dad. Bye.'

Greer had her fingers curled around the edge of the door. As Colby approached, she pulled back against the wall, to avoid any accidental physical contact as he left.

But he seemed in no hurry to go. 'How long have you had this place?' he asked, pausing as he came alongside.

'Almost four years now.'

'I like the way you've fixed it up. You've created a very relaxing ambience.'

'Well...thanks.'

'One bedroom, or two?'

'One.' Greer's gaze flicked to the door at Colby's left. 'May I?'

Before she could say no, he stepped over and pushed the door open. He stood in the doorway, silent for a moment as he looked around the small, sparsely furnished room.

'You surprise me.' He turned and walked back to her, his gaze speculative.

'In what way?'

'A single bed? I'd have thought...'

'Thought what?' Greer spoke lightly though she could feel the color seep from her face; she knew full well what he was implying.

He shrugged. 'A double...at the very least.' His tone was as light as her own, but his eyes had taken on a hooded knowing look with which she had become familiar.

'You mean for when I have someone...sleeping over?' She gave a tinkling laugh that was in direct contradiction to the way she was feeling. 'Don't let that worry you—the sofa in the sitting room folds out...it's actually a king-size hideabed. I'm prepared for every...contingency.'

'I wasn't worried—just puzzled. I like everything to be logical—I like to see everything fit together like the pieces of a jigsaw—and when I looked into your bedroom

I found myself wondering "What's wrong with this picture?"'

Nothing was wrong with the picture; it was *Colby's* picture of her that was all screwed up. She could have told him that...but instead she glanced at her watch, hoping he wouldn't notice how upset she was. 'It's getting late.'

When she looked up at him again, to her surprise, his expression had changed. He was frowning. What the devil was the matter now...?

'You look pale.' He put a hand on her forehead, and held it there. The tender pressure, and his closeness, brought the blood surging back into her face.

Colby's brows shot up. 'Must have been a trick of the light.' He let his hand drop. 'You look all right now—cheeks as red as roses. Right, I'm off...'

When he'd gone, Greer slammed the door shut behind him and leaned back against the wall, her eyes closed. How much longer could she go on like this? How much longer could she hide her true feelings for him? Because no matter how Colby needled her—and he had certainly been needling her when he implied she entertained men in her flat—when he'd had his hand on her brow, it was only by exercising supreme restraint that she'd kept herself from throwing her arms around his neck and—

The rain started, with a ferocity that startled her. It lashed against the windowpanes as if it wanted to wipe the apartment off the face of the earth. With a juddering sigh, Greer pushed herself upright and went through to join Jamie.

He was standing at the window.

'Dad was right.' His voice was awed. 'Golly gee, *what* a storm.'

Colby came back just before two.

When the intercom buzzer went, Jamie was curled up on the futon, watching TV and Greer was in the kitchen.

She pressed the button. 'Yes?'

'Colby.'

'Come on up.' Greer pressed the button that would open the door for him downstairs, and then took two ceramic mugs from the cupboard. 'Your dad's here,' she called to Jamie.

When there was no answer, she popped her head around the door. Jamie's gaze was fixed on a dinosaur tromping purposefully down a mountain toward a party of unsuspecting campers.

She crossed to stand between him and the set.

He glanced up.

'Your dad's here. Would you like to get the door when he knocks?'

'Sure.' Rolling off the futon, Jamie made for the adjoining hall, walking backward with his eyes fixed on the TV set.

Greer returned to the kitchen. As she opened the drawer to get a teaspoon, she caught a glimpse of herself in the chrome surface of the kettle...a distorted reflection of lemon blouse, blue jeans, pale hair, high cheekbones. How would she stack up, she wondered with a self-deprecatory grimace, against the nannies Colby had been interviewing?

She heard a brisk knock, heard Jamie open the door, heard the low rumble of a man's voice...and then Colby was in the kitchen, and the room seemed to shrink in his presence. Behind him, she could see Jamie on the futon again, gazing engrossingly at the continuing descent of the dinosaur.

'How did your day go?' Colby asked.

'Fine. And yours?'

'Mind if I take my jacket off? God, wasn't that rain something? It certainly cleared the air, but it's hotter than hell outside.' He stripped off his suit jacket, and flung it over the back of a chair. 'Do I smell coffee?'

'It's freshly made. Would you like a cup?'

He moved restlessly around the kitchen. 'Thanks.'

For a few moments, Greer busied herself with the coffeepot and mugs, but even after she gestured toward the table and said, 'Sit down,' Colby continued his restless prowling. Not that there was much space in which to prowl.

She gave him his coffee, and mug in hand, she leaned back against the countertop. 'So... did you find your Mary Poppins?'

He'd stopped prowling; had propped his hip on the edge of the small table. 'Two good possibilities. I've lined up second interviews today with both, so Jamie can meet them.' He took a deep swallow of his coffee. 'I was wondering if I could impose on you again, actually. Could you spare an hour or so to come downtown later on this afternoon?'

'You need someone to sit with Jamie while you have another private talk with the applicants?'

He shook his head. 'I thought it might be a good idea to have a woman's opinion before I make my final decision. Maybe you can pick up on something I might have missed.'

Mentally Greer juggled the schedule she'd worked out for the later part of her day. 'Sure, I can make time.'

'Thanks. I appreciate it.' From the fruit basket Greer kept in the center of the table, he absently plucked a ripe purple grape; just as absently popped it into his mouth, chewed it, swallowed. 'How did you keep Jamie occupied?'

'We took the subway downtown to an exhibition of Toys Through the Ages, which Jamie enjoyed. Then we had lunch at McDonald's—his choice, not mine!' She took a sip of her coffee. 'So... when's your first appointment?'

'Five. The second's an hour later.'

'Then I'll meet you there just before five. Jot down the address.' She ripped a page from the small pad she kept by the phone, and gave it to him.

He bent over the white-painted table as he wrote, and she felt her breath catch in her throat as she looked at his neck. She'd always loved the symmetrical way his hair grew at his nape, just as she loved the lithe lines of his upper body, the strong broad sweep of his shoulders. Her gaze moved to the ripple of muscle under his shirt as he wrote the address, and her eyes lingered, wistfully, yearningly...

'There.' Colby straightened, more quickly than she'd anticipated, and when he looked at her, his eyes narrowed. 'What?'

'What...what?' Her response was faint.

'What were you thinking?'

'Thinking?'

'Just now...your eyes were dreamy, distant...as if you were a thousand miles away.'

Greer felt the whip of sexual tension uncoil dangerously between them. 'I...was thinking about something I've got to do—someone I've got to see...at my workshop...in a little while.' She could tell, by Colby's tautening features, that he didn't believe her...that he knew her thoughts had been running along far different lines. Lines that interested him. Lines he intended to pursue. Cheeks flaming, she swiveled away and made for the door.

She'd almost reached it when he caught her arm with a firm hand; at the same time he hooked the door shut with his foot. The sharp click of the latch was almost drowned out by the screams of terror emanating from the TV set. The dinosaur, Greer thought dazedly, must be drawing close...but the panic bubbling inside those petrified campers could be no greater than the panic bubbling up inside herself. Helplessly she stared up at Colby...waiting...

'For God's sake don't look at me like that,' he said. 'I'm not going to bite! At least—' his voice had dropped a few notches, become intimate '—not unless you want me to.'

Oh, yes, she thought hysterically, I want you to...

Had he read her answer in her eyes? At any rate, he didn't give her time to finish the thought. He dragged her into his arms and claimed her lips in a kiss that frazzled her to the tips of her toes. When it was over, he released her as abruptly as he'd captured her, and she reeled back against the door, feeling as groggy as if he'd punched her.

'Yes,' he said softly, 'I see you do want me to bite you... and I shall take great pleasure in accommodating you in that regard. But this is neither the time nor the place.' He reached out and touched the pale hair splashed over her yellow top... and even in her dazed state, she could see that his fingers trembled, and the knowledge that he was not unaffected by their kiss set her heartbeats fluttering even more wildly. 'And it won't happen in any apartment kitchen,' he promised in thick honeyed tones. 'When we make love, I want to see this pale silk hair spread out over a goose-down pillow. I want you on your back, naked, with those beautiful green eyes wide open and moonlight turning your smooth creamy skin to silver...'

She wanted to cry 'Stop!' but her throat had become so tight she could scarcely breathe. All she was capable of doing was to slide away from the door, lean against the wall, gesture with a flailing hand that he should go and then wait for him to comply with her unspoken request.

He did. At last.

But first he scooped up his jacket, helped himself to a sprig of grapes and then demolished her last remaining defences with a smoldering gaze that promised there was a paradise ahead for them that was more rapturous than any she could even imagine.

As if from another planet, she heard Jamie click off the TV set, heard him call, 'See you later, Aunt Greer!' and then after a rustle of sound—Colby getting the anorak from the closet?—she heard the outside door open, and shut.

What a spineless creature I am, she thought as she sank to the floor and curled up in a despairing ball. She wanted never to see Colby Daken again...hadn't she told herself so, a hundred times since his return? Yet the thought of being in bed with him, the prospect of lying—moon-silvered and naked—in his arms the way he'd described...just the very thought made her body turn to mush. Good Lord, she couldn't even stand up—she had to sit here, boneless, like a pathetic little slave.

But that was all she wanted to be, at this moment. Colby Daken's slave. His sex slave.

And wasn't that what he wanted of her? Sex, but nothing else?

She dropped her brow onto her bent knees.

What on earth was she going to do!

The first nanny was a dead loss.

Greer didn't realize it at first. Crystal Malone was fresh from an excellent nanny training school and seemed to fit the bill. Brown-haired and ruddy-cheeked, she was cheerful, energetic, neatly dressed...and eminently likable. Greer found herself thinking, *This is the one*. But toward the end of the interview, Ms. Malone opened her purse to get a Kleenex and Greer—to her dismay—spotted a miniature liquor bottle peeping out from behind a navy wallet.

Wanting to give the prospective nanny the benefit of the doubt, Greer casually suggested they both pay a visit to the washroom before leaving. On the way back along the corridor, Greer pretended to trip, and stumbled against the other woman.

The faint but unmistakable smell of alcohol on Ms. Malone's breath confirmed her suspicions. She decided to keep what she'd found out to herself, till she got Colby alone.

When the interview was over and Ms. Malone had left, Colby shrugged out of his suit jacket and threw it down on a sofa by the window. He looked at his watch.

'We've twenty minutes before the next interview.' He glanced at Greer. 'What would you like to do?'

'I saw a park right across the street,' Jamie said. 'Could we go there?'

'Good idea.' Colby raised an enquiring eyebrow in Greer's direction. 'Okay?'

'Sounds good.'

The heat of the sun was intense, and Greer was glad she'd chosen to wear her airiest dress, a loose sleeveless affair in a cool shade of blue. The park was amply endowed with trees and the small group crossed toward a shaded spot under an enormous oak. Greer sat down on a wooden bench and stretched her legs out in front of her.

'Dad.' Jamie pointed to a nearby concession stand. 'What about an ice cream?'

'What *about* an ice cream?' Colby grinned. 'Want to rephrase your question?'

Jamie grinned back. 'Dad,' he said, in an exaggeratedly patient tone, 'would you and Aunt Greer like an ice cream? If you do, I'll go get them.'

Greer chuckled. 'He's a born diplomat, Colby.'

Colby slid his wallet from his hip pocket and extricated a couple of bills. 'What flavor for you, Greer?'

'Oh, I don't want one, thanks.'

'Sure?'

'Absolutely.'

'Okay. Jamie, make mine vanilla...here, that should be enough to cover it. And one scoop, okay?' He returned his wallet to his pocket. 'You don't want to spoil your appetite for dinner.'

As Jamie sped off, Greer said flatly, 'Ms. Malone's no good, Colby. She drinks.'

Colby didn't question her verdict, or ask her how she knew. Shaking his head, he just said, 'Good grief...and I thought...' Frustratedly he slackened the knot of his tie, and undid the top button of his shirt, angling his jaw up as he did in a move that was so quintessentially male it did strange wobbly things to Greer's insides.

Don't do that, she wanted to plead as she followed the movements of his fingers. Her gaze drifted to his throat, and the shadow of dusky hair just visible in the V of his shirt. *Can't you see what you're doing to me?*

She fixed her gaze instead on her sandals, a pair of Ferragamos she'd purchased in the spring...only to be guiltily reminded of another of her weaknesses: expensive Italian footwear. She sighed. 'We'll just have to keep our fingers crossed that the next one will be fine. If not, you'll have to go back to your short list.'

'Right.'

Silence settled between them, but it wasn't an awkward silence. Perhaps it was even companionable.

'All these new buildings,' Colby murmured. 'Toronto has changed a lot since I was here last.'

'Did you like Melbourne?'

He shrugged. 'Sure. But I'm glad to be back.'

'Your business there—Daken Construction—'

'I've already set things in motion to sell. I've a few buyers lined up. It'll be no problem.'

'Colby...' Greer hesitated and then went on. 'You must know that the high interest rates here have really chilled housing activity. Mortgage rates keep rising, financing is tight and shows no signs of improving. I don't mean to be negative, but surely this is a bad time for you to be starting up Daken Construction again here—'

'I plan on going into renovations. I'd already branched out successfully in that direction, in Melbourne, and I'm convinced that at the present time, it's the way to go. When the economy's strong, people feel confident enough to move up in the housing market and that generates a demand for new housing. When the economy's uncertain, as it is now, people are understandably nervous—they don't even know if they're going to have a job next month. So instead they tend to stay put and renovate—add another bedroom, build a solarium, modernize the kitchen.'

Greer felt a sense of relief. She should have known that Colby would have his business interests under control. 'Have you told Aunt Cecilia you're going to settle here?'

'I dropped her a note the other day.'

'Were she and Jamie close?'

Colby gave a cynical laugh. 'You know your aunt— or you used to. She hasn't changed. Never will. Can you imagine that woman having a warm relationship with *anyone?*'

'No,' Greer said truthfully. 'I certainly never felt close to her. And Gran knew what she was like. Gran told me that when Mom and Dad died, Aunt Cecilia offered to bring me up—'

'I can imagine the pious, self-sacrificing tone in which she made *that* offer!'

Greer smiled. 'Thank heaven Gran wanted to look after me. But I used to wish she didn't insist that because we were all family, we had to keep in touch. Those two weeks we used to spend with Aunt Cecilia every summer were the *pits!*'

'But you had your cousin...I always had the impression that you thought the world of—'

'Here, Dad. Your ice cream.'

Greer hadn't noticed Jamie approach; she was pretty sure Colby hadn't, either. But Jamie's timing was perfect; she didn't want to get into a discussion about Eleanor, or their relationship. Dangerous ground. Ground best avoided.

Jamie had chosen a chocolate ice cream for himself. He licked it as he gave Colby his cone, along with some change.

'Thanks.' Colby slipped the coins into his shirt pocket.

'May I go over to the swings?' Jamie asked.

'Sure—just stay where I can see you.'

Colby sat down beside Greer on the bench ... a bench that was about ten feet long, but as soon as he sat down, seemed to shrink to around four. Greer fought against an impulse to slide sideways, away from him.

'Want a lick?'

She turned to look at him. He was holding out his cone, and in his eyes there was a wicked twinkle.

She knew he expected her to refuse.

'Thanks,' she said lightly. 'Just a taste.'

She wasn't one to play games, but Colby Daken brought out the worst in her. Lips curved in a smile, with one hand she took hold of his wrist as if to steady it, and then she leaned forward toward the proffered cone. Flirting up at him from under her pale lashes, she allowed the tip of her tongue to glide over the confection's swirling peak, slowly, at the same time tightening her grip on his wrist. 'Mmm...'

The muscles of his forearm jerked as he flicked himself free and caught her fingers in a steely grip. 'That good, huh?' His eyes—suddenly as black as pitch—locked hers in a trap even more impossible to escape. 'My turn.'

He bent his head, his gaze never leaving hers, and—just as she had done a moment ago—licked the crest of the ice cream ... but with a deliberate intent that stimulated an immediate response in her breasts. She felt them tingle, tighten, swell...then felt something tug deep inside her, setting off an explosion of desire that rocketed through her, its heat charring every nerve ending in its path.

A shudder raked her body.

Colby's eyes widened in mock-surprise. 'Cold?' he drawled, his lips twitching. Releasing her, he sprawled back, his head tilted sideways so he could look at her.

'No.' A slight breeze moved the leafy branches above, allowing a ray of sunlight to peep its way down. It became trapped in Colby's hair, giving it the sheen of polished jet; Greer ached to ruffle it with her fingertips. She pasted on a casual smile. 'Actually I can hardly bear the heat.'

Colby's laugh was loud and spontaneous. 'We could start our own generator,' he said, with a provocative quirk of one eyebrow, 'and give Ontario Hydro a good run for its money.'

'Couldn't we just!' she said archly. 'If only we were so inclined.'

'Oh, I'm inclined.' He slid an arm along the back of the seat. She heard a slight rustle as his shirt brushed her dress, and at the same time she was subjected to his heady male scent. She stiffened. He licked his cone again, and rolled his eyes in a parody of ecstasy. 'I am indeed.'

'Well, what a pity,' Greer said with a curl of her upper lip, 'that I'm not.' She looked down at her watch, with every appearance of being cool, calm and collected. 'Oh, my,' she said, 'we'd better get going.'

She stood up and without waiting to see if Colby was following, started across the grass toward the swings.

It was just as well he couldn't see her face now, she thought, as she beckoned to Jamie. Her cheeks felt as if they were on fire. Her body felt as if it was on fire. Every single nerve ending and cell felt as if it was on fire. And if Colby could do that to her with a few words, a provocative lift of an eyebrow, and a mere brushing

of his shirt against her dress ... what on earth would he
do to her if he ever got her into his bed!

Alice Kerr was English, and had recently arrived in
Toronto. Her references were impeccable—her last post
had been with distant cousins of the British royal family
and they had recommended her most highly. She was
twenty-nine years old, a freckled redhead with an en-
gaging manner, and a forthright way of expressing herself
that impressed Greer right away.

When the interview was over, Colby told Ms. Kerr that
he'd call her next day, to let her know his decision.

After she left, he said to Greer, 'What do you think?'

'She seems perfect for the job.' Greer turned to Jamie.
'Did you like Miss Kerr, Jamie?'

'Yeah, she was okay.'

'Did you like her better than Miss Malone?' Colby
asked.

'Miss Malone smelled funny.' Jamie wandered over to
the window, and started watching the antics of two sea
gulls on a nearby ledge.

Colby said softly, 'Out of the mouths of babes.'

Greer chuckled. 'You didn't need me after all, did you!
So ... you'll hire her?'

'Yes. I'll call her tomorrow. I could have told her just
now ... I just wanted to make sure she met with your
approval.'

'She did. So,' Greer went on, 'all you need now is a
mistress. You want me to help you with that, too?'

Oh, Lord, where had those words come from! Why
did she have to spoil what had been a nice day by being
bitchy?

Colby stared down at her, as if he, too, was wondering
that same thing. 'No,' he said, 'I don't need any help
there. Do you need a drive?'

'No, I have my car.' Why did she feel this stab of disappointment? Had she expected that he would invite her

out to dinner? Not that she would have accepted, because she had to go back to her workshop...but after all, she *had* given up the best part of a day to accommodate him.

'Then that's settled.' He walked to the door and held it open for her. 'We're going back to the cottage tonight. We'll see you on the weekend.'

'No, I'm not coming up—'

He frowned. 'I'm sure Jem told me she was taking you to the Trillium Lodge on Saturday night. Am I mistaken?'

'I did tell Gran I'd go there some Saturday—but I hadn't realized she wanted to go *this* weekend.'

'She's counting on it.'

Dammit. 'Then,' Greer said, 'I *shall* see you at the cottage.' She turned to Jamie. 'Goodbye, Jamie. I really enjoyed our outing this morning.'

He pushed up his glasses. 'I had a fun time, too.'

'So see you Friday,' Colby said as she walked away. Without turning, she waved a vague hand out at her side, thankful he couldn't see her harried expression.

Destiny, it seemed, was determined to throw them together.

And who was she, to think she could challenge Fate and get away with it...but at least, she mused, she could throw out a defensive punch or two before succumbing.

She would find herself *very* busy on Friday—so busy she would have to phone Gran early and tell her she couldn't get away from her office till close to ten that night...and of course Gran would tell her that would be far too late to set out for the cottage on her own. She would agree meekly, and arrange to arrive at the lake on Saturday.

CHAPTER NINE

ON SATURDAY, the air in Toronto was as stale and bronzed as yesterday's toast, the sidewalks hot enough to melt butter.

Greer was glad to get away. Ironically she'd been forced by pressure of work to stay at the office till after eleven the night before, and had been so stressed by the time she got home she couldn't sleep. But on the drive north, she began to relax, and by the time she got to Barrie, she was actually humming along with the music on the radio.

On arrival at the lake, however, Colby materialized even before she'd shut the car door behind her, and her tension automatically snapped into place again.

He was wearing only a pair of black swim trunks, slung carelessly low on his hips, and with his deep tan and leanly muscled physique, he could have stepped from the cover of a 'Hunks of the Year' calendar. Greer scolded herself for wanting to let her gaze wander, and fixed it on his face—but it wasn't safe there, either. Pinned by eyes bluer than the sky, she felt as breathless as if he'd kissed her.

Tucking a large brown paper bag of groceries against her hip, she pushed her car door shut. 'Hi.'

'Lookin' good, Greer.' Unlike her own, Colby's gaze had apparently been granted free rein. As it skimmed over the generous expanse of flesh exposed by her tank top and short shorts, Greer felt her traitorous nerves respond with a delighted shiver. 'How was the drive?'

'Not bad,' she said... and in retaliation, she let her own gaze loose, directing it impudently over him from tip to toe, before locking eyes with him again. She raised a mocking brow. 'Not bad at all!'

A twinkle starred his pupils. 'Touché.'

'So... what do you want, Colby—no.' She hurried to correct herself as his lips twitched. 'Let me rephrase my question. Did you have something you want to say to me?'

'Jem has gone into Parry Sound with Lisa and the girls. She asked me to tell you they'll be back around two.'

'Thanks.' Greer hugged the grocery bag against her breasts like a shield. 'Where's Jamie?'

'He and Chris are painting some planks for me. I've been fixing the boathouse wall and hammered the last nail just a minute ago. I came over to get us some cold drinks.' He ran a hand over his hair-roughened chest. 'Fancy something?'

Oh, yes, she thought. Indeed yes. *You.* And she'd better keep out of his way if she didn't want him to sense her weakness and act on it. In Toronto, fully clothed, he'd been able to make her melt with a mere brushing of shirt against dress; in his present half-clad state he could reduce her to ashes at ten paces if he set his mind to it.

'Well?' His voice obtruded into her thoughts.

She braced herself against his magnetism. 'No, thanks. I... feel like being on my own for a bit.'

'Rough week?'

'Busy.'

'A swim,' he said, 'would relax you. I was planning to go for a dip myself once I've attended to my painting crew. Get your bikini on—I'll meet you out on the float.'

Greer frowned. 'I really don't—'

'Something's happened.' All at once there was no twinkle in his eye, no amusement in his expression. He looked grim. 'I need to talk to somebody... blow off steam.'

He strode away, leaving Greer standing there, uncertain. What could possibly be wrong? Was it Jamie?
Had he retreated into his shell again? No, that wouldn't
have provoked the kind of anger she sensed in Colby.

Lost in thought, she walked slowly to the cottage and
into the kitchen. When she opened the fridge to put away
the perishables she'd bought, she saw Jem had prepared
a jug of iced tea. She filled a glass and took it through
to the bedroom with her, snatching the odd sip of the
chilled drink while she freshened up and changed into
a bikini.

A few minutes later, she was in the water, swimming
with long steady strokes to the float.

'Eleanor's mother has started legal proceedings to get
custody of Jamie.'

Greer was sitting cross-legged on the float; she looked
up at Colby disbelievingly as his terse announcement
sank in. 'No!' She pressed a hand against her collarbone
as her heartbeats jarred raggedly. 'When did you find
out?'

'My lawyer phoned yesterday.' The sun was at Colby's
back and she couldn't see his eyes, but his harsh tone
revealed that he was barely containing a swelling fury.

'But why?' Greer scrambled to her feet. 'What reason
could Aunt Cecilia possibly have for—'

Colby's mouth twisted grimly. 'This is a direct response to my note telling her I'd be settling here.'

'Well, yes, she'll miss her grandson, of course... and
I can understand how your news must have upset her.
But to try to get *custody*? Surely she doesn't have a leg
to stand on! You're Jamie's father, after all, and she's
only—'

'Your aunt accuses me of being a workaholic, says I
put my own needs before the needs of my child. And
because I've taken him away from his familiar sur-

roundings, she's accused me of not providing a stable environment. She says—'

Greer cut him off with a sharp dismissive gesture. 'What does your *lawyer* say? It's not the first time this kind of custody battle has happened. He must have some experience as to how to deal with it. Surely he doesn't think Aunt Cecilia has a chance?'

'Fact is I *did* put my work first in recent years, and dammit, I *didn't* see as much of Jamie as I should have...'

Greer sensed an odd tension in him, and it made her uneasy. When she noticed he was no longer meeting her eyes, she felt her uneasiness increase. *What was Colby not telling her?* Something, she was sure. He had admitted he had neglected Jamie, and that in itself was bewildering; she *knew* he wasn't the kind of man to do such a thing. So what on earth could have caused him to—

'My lawyer has warned me that in a case like mine,' Colby said flatly, 'the decision can go either way, depending on the judge. He also advised me there is probably only one route I can take if I want to make absolutely sure I get to retain custody.'

'What's that?'

He turned from Greer, the muscles in his shoulders bunched. 'He says I should find myself a wife.' He lashed out with a tight fist. 'I don't *want* to get married again.'

Legs shaky, Greer walked to the far end of the float, and stared out over the lake.

Why did life have to be so difficult she wondered. Why was it that when one problem was solved, another seemed to erupt to take its place? As surely as she knew Colby loved Jamie, she also knew he'd do everything in his power to keep his son. How torn he must feel. She felt as if her own heart, too, were being torn. She hugged her arms around herself—realized she was shivering, despite the heat of the sun. Oh, if only there was some way she could help...

She turned, to find Colby was still gazing out over the water. 'What are you going to do?' she asked.

There was a long... agonizingly long... pause before he turned around. 'I'll find somebody.'

'You mean—' her voice was weak '—you will marry, just to keep Jamie?'

'Not *just*, Greer! Never say *just* to keep Jamie, as if he weren't worth—'

'Oh, I didn't mean that—you know I didn't—'

'Yes, I'd marry if it meant keeping my son. And I'd marry for no other reason. But where, in the name of heaven, am I to...' His voice trailed away, as if he had become so lost in his problem he was no longer conscious of Greer's presence.

And as the silent moments ticked by, an idea—an *outrageous* idea—swooped into Greer's head, and as immediately as it did, she rejected it. Rejected it violently. No! she could *not* do it; she would not do it. A strange trembling reverberated in her soul, as if an earthquake had shuddered through her. What was she thinking! How could she possibly even consider such an idea! Yet hadn't she just moments ago ached to be able to help Colby? Hadn't she wondered, despairingly, if there was something she could do? Well, there *was* something... but reaction to her own solution was only now setting in, and she felt faint... but she forced her mind to stick with it.

She *could* be the one, the one to marry Colby. Surely that would be the way out, the only way out, of his dilemma? For after all, speed was of the essence in this battle with Cecilia, and where else would Colby find someone at such short notice who would be willing to enter into a marriage with him?

Someone who would make no demands?

Greer cleared her throat. 'You...don't have...anybody in mind? Some old friend, perhaps, who—'

'I don't have women friends,' he snapped. 'I look to my own sex for friendship. I look to women for—' He stopped abruptly, closed his eyes briefly, flicked a hand out, palm up, in apology. 'Sorry. To answer your question, no, I don't have a female friend to help me out here.'

'We used to be friends.'

He stared at her blankly. 'What does that have to do with anything?'

'I'll do it, Colby.'

'*What?*'

'I'll marry you...or at least, go through the motions. I'll put on a show, for the judge, for Aunt Cecilia, for anyone else you think it's important to—'

'*No!*'

'Why not? I would make no demands—it would be a simple thing for us to write up a mutually agreeable contract beforehand. To all intents and purposes, we could go on living separate lives...but of course we would have to live in the same house...at least, for the time being—'

'Didn't you hear me?' Colby grasped her shoulders, hard, and she could tell, by the tension pulsating between them, that he was only by a thread managing to maintain control of his emotions. 'I said—'

'Hey, Dad, we're finished!'

Jamie's shout from the beach acted like a pistol shot. Colby released her abruptly, and she lost her balance. She'd been standing close to the edge of the float; now she found herself tumbling backward into space...and into the water. She hit it with a loud splash.

When she surfaced, spluttering, it was to see Colby looking down at her from the float, his expression strained.

'Dammit, Greer, I didn't mean to—you okay?'

Greer swept her wet ponytail back over her shoulders. 'Think about what I said,' she gasped, treading water. 'But it's a time-limited offer—expires at midnight. As I see it—' she rubbed her eyes to clear her vision, and noticed that his face was very pale '—I'm your only option. But remember, I'd be doing it for Jamie, not for his father.'

As she struck out for the beach, she threw over her shoulder, 'You're the *last* man I would choose to marry.'

Jem arrived home shortly before two, but when she confessed why she'd gone to Parry Sound, Greer reacted with dismay.

'You went to see a doctor? Gran, what on earth's—'

'Oh, don't fuss!' Jem waved her cane airily. 'Pour me a glass of water, dear.' She sank onto a kitchen chair.

Greer hurried to do her bidding. 'Tell me what's wrong, Gran,' she said. 'Please.'

Jem took a sip of the water, before placing the glass on the table in front of her. 'My stomach started acting up again yesterday, so I asked Lisa this morning if she'd take me to the clinic. The doctor said it's nothing serious, just the tail end of whatever ailed me last week. He's given me some pills and I'm to be careful of what I eat for the next few days.' She lifted one shoulder in a dismissive shrug. 'That's all. Nothing to get excited about.'

'But why didn't you call me yesterday? You know I'd have driven straight up here and looked after you!'

'I thought about it, but then you phoned and said you were going to be awfully busy and wouldn't be finished work till quite late.'

Greer felt a stab of guilt. If she hadn't been playing games with Colby—hadn't deliberately planned to stay in town just to avoid him—this wouldn't have happened. 'I'm sorry, Gran. But if I'd known you were feeling poorly I'd have dropped everything—'

'Of course you would, and that's why I didn't want to bother you. There's only one thing, though...'

'And what's that?'

'Our booking at the Lodge. I want a poached egg and toast for dinner tonight, and I'm certainly not going to pay the inflated prices they charge there, for something I can perfectly well cook at home. So—'

'No problem. I'll phone and cancel—'

'No need to do that. I was talking with Colby just now, asked him if he'd like to take my place and he said it would be his pleasure. He'll come over around seven. And Lisa has invited Jamie to a sleepover, so you won't have to rush home. Now.' Jem pushed her chair back and got to her feet. 'I'm going to have a siesta. The doc told me it was time I started to slow down, and I'm going to take his advice.'

Outraged at her grandmother's high-handed reshuffling of their arrangements, Greer opened her mouth to splutter out an indignant protest, but before she could, Jem added, with a twinkle in her eyes, 'The doc also told me to avoid confrontations as stress would aggravate my condition.' She turned and *tap-tapped* her way out of the kitchen.

Greer bit back a frustrated oath, and as she did, she heard a muffled titter out in the hallway. So...Jemima Westbury was amused that she'd sly maneuvered an intimate dinner at the Lodge for two of her favorite people.

What would the wily old bird think, Greer wondered, if she knew her beloved granddaughter had only hours ago offered herself in marriage to Colby Daken...

And been flatly rejected.

Colby called for Greer a few minutes before seven.

She and Jem were out on the veranda when he arrived. Her grandmother had been arranging flowers in a vase—wildflowers Jamie had brought her earlier, 'for the invalid,' he'd said with a blush. Jem was just saying to Greer, 'What a *sweet* child he is—there's a wealth of love inside that boy, just *waiting* to be tapped,' when purposeful footsteps hit the veranda stairs, and Greer knew her date was here.

As usual, at the sight of Colby she was almost overwhelmed by a surge of yearning. Tonight he was wearing a navy linen pin-stripe suit along with an open-necked shirt in a lighter navy; his belt buckle was silver, and the glint of metal drew her gaze down to his pleated trousers...and to his lean hips, his powerful thighs. Her breath caught in her throat and throwing up a prayer for strength, she raised her gaze.

His eyes were disturbingly dark, the wide dilation of his pupils revealing to Greer that he found her just as desirable as she found him. The knowledge made her giddy. Yet when he spoke, it was in a tone of cool amusement that on the surface at least belied such a notion.

Shaking his head, he regarded her with a faint smile. 'Wherever did she go,' he asked, hands in pockets and rocking back on his heels, 'that scrappy tomboy with the cheeky grin and the bruised knees and the cropped hair?'

Greer had chosen to wear one of her own creations, an emerald green tank top dress of a rich rib-knit silk that clung attractively to her feminine curves, and she knew she'd never looked better. Yet under Colby's ironic gaze, she felt reduced inside to adolescent gawkiness.

'That girl?' she returned dryly. 'She's long gone...except for her scrappiness. And thank heavens that's still there—she certainly needs it when she's around you.'

He laughed. 'We've got the makings of a charming evening here. And—' he glanced at his watch '—we'd better get that evening started. It'll take us a while to walk to the Lodge, and we'll want to have a drink at the bar before we eat. Ready?'

'Mmm.' Greer kissed her grandmother. 'Bye, Gran.'

'Goodbye, both,' Jem said. 'Have a lovely time.'

After they'd gone, Jem stood for a while, leaning against the table, lost in thought. Then she plucked a red poppy from her vase of wildflowers, and stuck it jauntily in her topknot. Unhooking her cane from the back of a chair, she moved slowly across to the railing.

She looked up at the heavens, her eyes questioning.

'That's it, then,' she said, in the companionable voice she'd have used to a close friend. 'I've done *my* bit. The rest is up to you.

'Just see you don't make a botch of it.'

The Trillium Lodge's cocktail lounge hummed with activity. The majority of seats were taken, with chattering patrons comfortably ensconced in cushioned armchairs around low round walnut tables. Other guests were perched on high stools at the curved bar, and several more were standing in clusters in front of it. The scents permeating the air spelled luxury, Greer decided as she and Colby paused in the wide doorway and she inhaled the elusive hints of French perfume and expensive aftershaves; the heady fragrance of roses mingling with the pleasant aroma of good wines—

Colby drew her to one side as two couples passed by, and Greer noticed that the women stared with openly covetous expressions at Colby. If *he* noticed, he paid them no heed. Cupping Greer's elbow, he led her forward into the lounge.

'There's a good spot,' he murmured, nodding toward a table being vacated over by the fireplace. 'Shall we...?'

As they made their way through the crowd, Greer noticed that other women's heads were turning as Colby passed. It was no surprise, because he was the most attractive man in sight... but for some reason it pleased her immensely that he seemed unaware of the ripple of attention he was causing.

So taken up was she with her thoughts, she was startled when Colby stopped, just before they reached their table. She blinked, and realized someone—a man—had waylaid him.

'Colby Daken?' The stranger—distinguished-looking, with gray hair and gray eyes—searched Colby's face. 'It *is* you, isn't it? You won't remember me, of course, but—'

'Of course I remember you.' Colby's voice was warm. 'Zach Grantham. You were my father's partner, back in the old days, before you both decided to go your separate ways.'

With pleased laughter, the men shook hands. Zach Grantham, Greer mused, had the unmistakable look of someone with money...though there was nothing ostentatious about him. The glint of his gold watch was dull; the color of his suit, which was unmistakably an Armani, was subdued; even the pattern of his silk tie was discreet.

'It's great to see you, Zach,' Colby was saying. He turned to Greer. 'Greer, I'd like you to meet Zach Grantham. Zach—Greer Alexander. Greer's grandmother owns the next cottage to mine, a mile or so along the beach.'

Greer offered her hand, and Zach clasped it firmly.

'A pleasure,' he said, his eyes twinkling. 'It always is, to meet a beautiful woman, even at my advanced age.'

'Zach and Dad were buddies when they were growing up, Greer, and—' he addressed Zach '—you were both widowed early so you had a lot in common even when you were older.'

'That we did. Although I did eventually marry again, but—ah, excuse me.' Zach's eyes softened as he looked over Colby's shoulder. 'Here she is, the love of my life.'

Greer followed the man's doting gaze and saw a sultry-looking brunette gliding toward them, her overblown curves accentuated by a clinging fuchsia minidress. Greer gulped. Zach Grantham looked to be about seventy; his wife was maybe in her late twenties. Talk about May/September marriages!

When the woman reached them, she flicked a dismissive gaze over Greer and turned her attention to Colby. As she did, she gasped, and her brown eyes became slumberous. She fixed them on him with the welcoming glow of bedroom lamps. 'My God!' Her throaty purr was so brazenly provocative it had the hair on Greer's nape standing on end. 'It can't be you! Colby Daken, my first love. Oh, honey—'

Stunned, Greer watched as the stranger launched herself at Colby. Weaving her fuchsia-tipped fingers into his hair, she looked up at him adoringly, her fuchsia-painted lips parted, her alabaster skin spangled by the glittering lights from the bar. Her prominent breasts were squashed hard against Colby's chest, and Greer could only imagine how his body was responding to such a blatantly erotic invitation.

Hating herself for being unable to contain her avid curiosity, she stole a quick look at his face... and felt as if the blades of a Mixmaster was churning the contents of her stomach. Colby's expression, as he grinned down at this woman, was wolfish; there was no other way to describe it. Like a rapacious, flesh-devouring animal, he was eating her with his eyes... and enjoying every succulent mouthful.

'Well,' he drawled, 'if it isn't Bettina Boom-boom Grantham—'

Bettina Boom-boom Grantham pulled his head down and kissed him.

Greer felt as if a vacuum was sucking all the breath from her lungs. Lord, what a kiss! The air positively sizzled with it! And with every second that passed, Greer felt her heart sink another notch.

But this Bettina Boom-boom—and what a disgusting nickname *that* was; what did it tell a person about *her*

morals!—was married! Covertly, Greer glanced at
Zach... only to find to her bewilderment that he was
watching them indulgently.

But when the clinch ended, he said, 'Honey, if you
could just restrain yourself for a moment, I'd like to ask
Colby what he's been doing with himself these past
years—I'd like to know if he's still in the construction
business.'

Bettina pouted. 'Oh, Daddy, you always want to talk
about business. It's so *boring!*'

Daddy? Not hubby? And Colby had been this bimbo's
first love? Greer hoped her expression showed nothing
of her distaste as Zach introduced her to the brunette.

'Greer, this is my daughter, Bettina. As you can see,
I've spoiled her rotten... my only excuse being she's all
I have left, since my second wife Dorothy passed away
a few years back. Betti, this is Colby's friend, Greer
Alexander.'

'Delighted,' Bettina murmured, barely glancing at
Greer before she turned back to Colby again. 'So, honey,
tell Daddy what you've been up to all this time.'

While Colby filled Zach Grantham in, Bettina hung
onto Colby's arm and his every word. And when Colby,
in turn, wanted to hear what Zach had been doing, the
brunette still kept her gaze on Colby as if she were a
mesmerized rabbit.

Greer, on the other hand, concentrated on what the
older man was saying; he included her in the conversation and she was genuinely interested in hearing about
the chain of superb hotels he owned, all over North
America.

It was the first time she'd ever seen Colby talk business,
and as she watched the two men, both wearing the indefinable aura of power and self-assurance that success
had brought, she couldn't help feeling in awe of them.

'Greer?'

She realized Colby was addressing her. 'Mmm? Sorry?'

'I think we should be getting along.' He glanced at his watch. 'If we want to have that drink before dinner.'

'Oh... yes.' She forced a smile. 'Fine.'

Zach nodded. 'And we have to be hitting the road. Pity we couldn't have dined together, Colby.' The men shook hands. 'I'll be in touch. I hope I'll be able to throw some business your way, now you're back in the country.'

Bettina fingered one of Colby's lapels lingeringly as she gave him a smoldering look from under her mascara-laden lashes. 'We'll have you round to the house, honey, soon...'

After the Granthams left, Greer turned toward the table they'd been making for, but Colby stopped her. 'I think,' he said, 'we ought to have our drink in the dining room. That little encounter has thrown our schedule off a bit, and our table will be waiting. Sorry about that.'

Greer shrugged her shoulders airily. 'No apology necessary—I wouldn't have missed it for the world. It was very... interesting... to see the kind of female you ran around with when you were younger.' She tilted her head, and with a malicious little smile, whisked his handkerchief from his breast pocket, and breezily wiped two thick smudges of fuchsia lipstick from his mouth.

'There.' She rammed the soiled handkerchief back into his pocket, knowing she had taken him aback, and enjoying his blank stare. 'That's better.' Over her shoulder she added, as she started walking toward the door, 'I have to tell you, *honey,* fuchsia is *not* one of your best colors.'

An hour and a half later, after a wonderful dinner of salad, fresh lobster and a sinfully rich chocolate cheesecake adorned with wild white strawberries, Colby sipped the last drop from his coffee cup, put the cup down in its saucer and looked squarely across the dining table at Greer.

She met his gaze, and inwardly winced. They had spoken barely two words to each other over the meal—*her* fault, she admitted to herself guiltily, because every time he'd tried to start up a conversation, she'd cut him off tersely.

'You're sulking,' he now remarked in a mild tone, though his eyes had a taunting glint. 'I do believe you were...miffed...because Bettina kissed me.'

'Pul-lease!' Greer whipped her napkin from her lap and flung it down onto her side plate. She glared at him as if he were a marauding beetle. 'Why should it bother me to see you make a fool of yourself with a bimbo called Boom-boom!'

He tilted his chair back lazily, and surveyed her from under hooded eyelids. 'I don't know,' he murmured. 'But if *that's* not why you're being so bitchy, then why—'

He broke off with a frown, and Greer realized he was looking at something—or someone—behind her. She saw his frown deepen, saw him jerk his chair up straight. His eyes were no longer hooded, but narrowed. What...?

Just as she was about to turn and investigate, Greer sensed that somebody had come up right behind her chair, but before she could swivel around, she felt warm smooth hands go over her eyes, firmly. A man's hands, she could tell that by their size and strength—

'What...?' she sputtered. 'Who...?'

'Guess.' There was amusement in the baritone voice. A voice she recognized right away.

'Nick.' She chuckled delightedly as she pulled his hands away. 'Nick Westmore.' She looked up and it was indeed, Nick Westmore. She hadn't seen him in three years, since he'd moved west to take up a post at Vancouver General, but he hadn't changed much...unless he was even more handsome than before. *If* that was possible.

She got to her feet, and Nick enfolded her in a warm hug that she returned enthusiastically. Tilting her head, she looked up at him. 'What a *lovely* surprise!'

'Ditto!' His hazel eyes twinkled down at her, the tips of his long fingers rested casually on her hips. 'And you, my love, are more beautiful than ever. If only this weren't a public place—' He grinned. 'Oh, what the heck.'

He lowered his head and kissed her.

Greer remembered his kisses. They had been sweet, and purposeful, and loving. She had enjoyed them...but not enough. Never enough. Never enough to blot out her memories of Colby. She stifled a sigh. *Nothing* had changed.

As Nick drew back, and she chided him affectionately for the public display, she heard Colby clearing his throat. There was more than an edge of irritation to the sound.

With one of Nick's arms still around her, she turned, to find that Colby had got up from his seat and was right beside her. His brows were drawn down in a scowl.

'Oh...Nick, I'd like you to meet Colby Daken. Colby.' Oh, Lord, she knew she was being wicked but she couldn't resist. 'This is my *very* first love, Nick Westmore.'

Perfunctorily the men shook hands. Then before Colby could say anything, she said, 'Nick...*honey*...would you like to sit down and have a coffee with us?'

If Nick thought it strange that she addressed him as 'honey,' he showed no sign of it. But his eyes did darken with disappointment. 'I wish I could, but I'm with my brother—we're on our way to Huntsville, to pick up his wife.' He raked a hand through his blond hair, straightened a tie that didn't need straightening. 'Greer.' His voice had dropped to an intimate level, but not so low that Colby couldn't have heard. 'Speaking of wives...are you married?'

'No.' Greer hid a smile. 'I'm not.'

'You're still in the apartment off Yonge?'

'The same.'

He grinned again. 'I've just moved back to Toronto. How about if I give you a call soon and we'll have dinner?'

'I'd like that.'

'Wonderful.' Nick grasped her shoulders lightly and brushed a kiss over her brow. Then after holding back her chair so she could be seated again, he threw Colby a casual 'See you around, Colby' and strode away, with as much confidence and energy in his step as Colby ever had in his.

Greer sank back in her chair. Nick was such a sweetie, but of course he was not for her. Colby, though, need never know that.

'What a nice man,' she murmured, playing idly with her crumpled napkin. 'Such a clever one, too—he's a surgeon now, one of the best in the country, I believe. But he's not only brilliant, he's also sophisticated and charming to boot. Of course, I've always had a weakness for *blond* men—they have a certain *je ne sais quoi* that dark men lack. I'm so glad he's back in town. Yes...' She allowed her tone to become slightly amused but thoughtful as she added, 'Nick Westmore is *quite* a catch.'

She snuck a look at Colby under her lashes, and saw that his lips were so tightly compressed they were almost white.

'If the man is such a catch,' he said icily, 'why ever did you let him get away? I got the impression from what he said that you were the one who broke off the relationship. What was the problem?' He fisted his hands hard on the table—rattling his cup and saucer—and leaning forward with a sneer on his face, hissed, *'Couldn't he satisfy you?'*

Outraged, Greer dug her elbows hard into the linen tablecloth, on either side of *her* cup and saucer, and lacing her fingers so tightly together under her chin that it hurt, leaned forward, too, so that she was eye to scathing eye with him. 'Well, I gathered you were the one to break off your relationship with Bettina Boom-boom Grantham! What was *your* problem, *honey?*' She hoped her scornful smile would wither him. *'Weren't you able to keep up with her?'*

For several long moments they glared at each other, their anger almost palpable. And then, even as Greer tried to steady the erratic thumping of her heartbeats, she suddenly saw the humor of the situation. What would Jem think now, she wondered, if she could see how her wily maneuverings had turned out.

Hysterical laughter bubbled up in her throat, and to her amazement, at the exact moment when she could contain her merriment no longer and it erupted in a paroxysm of uncontrollable schoolgirl giggles, she saw Colby's face crease in a reluctant smile, a smile that slowly gathered momentum, and ended up in a low rumble of laughter that came from somewhere very deep in his chest.

'If Jem could see us now,' he said, his eyes brimming with amusement as he watched Greer press a bunched-up Kleenex against her mouth in a futile attempt to stifle her helpless giggles, 'she'd empty that—' he nodded toward the elegant coffeepot sitting on the table '—over our heads.'

The laughter broke the tension that had been sparking between them all evening. Agreeing to salvage what was left of their night out, they called a truce. Colby ordered a fresh pot of coffee, and liqueurs—Drambuie for himself, Tia Maria for Greer—and they sat on, chatting about books they'd read, movies they'd seen, CDs they'd bought... till at last Greer looked at her watch and said with a sigh, 'We really ought to go. It's getting late...'

The moon was bright, and the air still warm when they walked together down the steps from the Lodge. And perhaps because of the wine she'd drunk, and the

Tia Maria, Greer found herself drifting into a dreamy mood as she and Colby strolled back along the beach—the kind of mood she hadn't indulged in for longer than she cared to remember.

She'd always loved being out of doors on a summer's night...she loved the way the air smelled differently than it did during the day, as if the last rays of the setting sun laced it with mystery and primal secrets. But what she loved more than anything was the spellbound feeling that invariably held her in its thrall when she looked up at the starry sky. She always became lost in wonder as she tried to grapple with the eternal conundrum of what lay beyond—

'Greer.'

Colby's voice cut into her drifting reverie. She turned, and saw he had stopped walking. She stopped, too.

'Mmm?' As she looked at him, she felt dazzled; the moonlight had transformed his face into a charcoal and white portrait of stark male beauty. How she wished she were a skilled portraitist, to capture the picture forever.

'About your proposal...'

His words brought Greer back to earth with a solid thump. She stared at him, feeling disoriented. She'd forgotten all about her proposal, and assumed he had, too. He'd made it quite clear, that morning, that it was of no interest to him. Why would he bring it up again now?

He rammed his hands into his trouser pockets, and fixed her with a gaze that was totally unreadable. 'I accept.'

'You...what did you say?' Greer wondered if he'd really said what she thought he had, or if she was still spellbound by the magic of the summer night. 'Did you—'

'We'll get married.'

A cool wind gusted from the lake, making Greer shiver. She rubbed her arms, unable to collect her thoughts. But as she struggled to cope with the implications of what Colby had just said, he shrugged off his linen jacket.

'Here.' He slipped it over her shoulders, and the silk lining brushed her bare arms. 'You're cold.' The fabric still held the warmth of his body—it also held his own familiar scent, and the erotic combination affected Greer as if it were some intoxicating drug, making her legs weak.

'Thanks.' She closed her eyes for a brief moment as Colby flicked out heavy strands of pale hair that had become trapped at her nape. Things were moving too fast, she acknowledged in a panic. Where did they go from here?

'You did say your offer would stand till midnight— I'm not too late, am I?' Gold glinted as he pushed up his shirt cuff. 'No, I still have several minutes left. But you seem stunned by my acceptance. Do you ... want to back out?'

Greer curled her fingers around the jacket's lapels. She felt her heartbeats jumble together as if they'd forgotten their rhythm and were struggling to find it again. She resumed walking, keeping her gaze fixed on the lights of the cottages ahead. 'No,' she said. 'I won't back out.'

Silence settled between them again as they walked on, but it was no longer the easy silence they'd shared earlier. It was a silence fraught with tension and it lasted for several minutes. Greer was the one who broke it this time.

'We'll have to make plans.' Her voice was strained.

'We'll have to tell Jem.'

'I'll tell her. I'll want to ... explain.'

He paused a beat, and then said quietly, 'Yes, that might be best. But for the others ... just an announcement. No explanations.'

'What do we say?' There was a trace of irony in Greer's tone. 'That we suddenly realized we were madly, passionately in love with each other?'

'That's what everyone will assume.' If the abrupt change in her tone had jarred Colby, his calm response showed no sign of it. 'I'll have a talk with Jamie in the morning...play it down, I think, till he gets used to the idea...though I don't anticipate any problem. He does like you. So if it's all right with you, we should get married as soon as possible, and stop Cecilia dead in her tracks.'

'Yes.'

'A small wedding?'

All at once Greer was hit by a delayed reaction. In vain she tried to gain control of the thoughts that were swirling around, making her head spin. *She was going to marry this man.* Over and over, like a broken record, the words repeated themselves. *She was going to marry Colby Daken.* It was unbelievable...the fantasies of her teenage years were going to come true. At last. But in a way she could never, in her wildest imaginings, have anticipated—

'Greer...a quiet wedding?'

As Colby's voice nudged her scattered thoughts, they coalesced and she was able to think clearly again.

'Not so quiet. I intend getting married only once. I shall want my friends to share the day.' She drew strength from his surprise, and courage from the knowledge that she'd thrown him off balance. 'And I want a white wedding.'

She sensed Colby do a double-take, but she kept her gaze fixed on the cottage lights. When he spoke again, it was in a careful tone. 'Historically white is for...virgins.'

'It's my wedding, Colby.' She was glad the night was shadowy; he wouldn't be able to see the pain in her eyes. 'I'll decide what I'm going to wear.'

'A white wedding it is then. Actually it should impress the hell out of the judge, and be in my favor. Appearances are everything.'

Oh, Colby, Greer thought unhappily, how wrong you
are. But she didn't argue the point. How could she? She
might give too much away.

'Greer, I'm curious... what do *you* expect to get out
this marriage?'

I expect to get the bittersweet pleasure of seeing you
every day, she wanted to cry... and I expect to endure
the pain of sleepless nights spent alone, weeping for
something I can't have... your love.

'A ready-made son, Colby, an endearing child who
has already found his way into my heart. Other than
that...very little. I have a career, a life of my own, friends
of my own... all of which I intend to keep. Of course
I'll give up my flat—I imagine you'll want to provide
your family with a house—'

'A house? Why not a...*home?*'

'A home is something else.' Emotion made Greer's
voice husky. 'It's not something you buy... or build. A
home comes from... the giving and sharing of love.'

'I love my son.' His face shadowed for the moment,
Colby's eyes were reduced to glinting slits in his dark
hard-angled face. 'And I do believe that love is returned.'

'But you dislike me, so no matter how much Jamie
and I may grow to love each other, there will always be
a thread of discord between you and me that will prevent
our being able to create a real home.'

They had reached the grassy patch just below the
Daken cottage, and they stopped, under the gracefully
cascading branches of an old willow tree. The moon
glimmered among the green leaves as if it were silently
falling silver pennies, sending narrow beams glancing
over their faces.

'I don't dislike you, Greer—I only dislike the way you
have   sometimes   behaved.   So...when   we   get
married—' Colby's hands were suddenly curved around
her shoulders, and to Greer's surprise, she felt his fingers
tremble '—it will be a proper marriage. A real marriage,

and our house *will* be a home. But the only way that
can happen is if we put the past behind us. Start afresh.
But.' His fingers tightened, digging almost painfully into
her bare flesh. 'If you ever so much as look at another
man, I'll—'

'No!' Horrified as what he was saying finally seeped
into her muddled brain, Greer jerked back from him,
and found herself pressed hard against the trunk of the
willow tree. 'I thought you understood... what I was
offering was a marriage in name only...for Jamie's sake!'

He slammed his hands, palm down, on the tree trunk,
on either side of her head. 'When we get married,' his
voice had a grating quality that sent a skitter of apprehension through her, 'it will be a marriage in every sense
of the word. We'll be making vows, and by God, I'll
expect us both to keep them. From you, I shall expect
nothing less than total commitment... which is what I,
in turn, shall be giving you.'

He framed her face in his hands, and with her swift
intake of breath, she drew in the fragrance of dry bark
on his fingers. He angled his lower body against hers,
the unyielding sensual pressure of his thighs against her
flesh stimulating a spasm of aching response. He lowered
his head slowly, his breath fanning her eyes, her lips,
her neck.

And he kissed her. Thoroughly. Possessively. And in-
timately. By the time he'd finished, her lips were bruised,
her body crushed, her lungs desperate for air. But the
conflagration of desire he'd kindled inside her was like
nothing she'd experienced before.

When finally he pulled back, his harsh breathing revealed that he was as aroused as she was. But she'd had
more concrete proof of his arousal just seconds before.
And when she'd become aware of it she'd felt more terrified than she'd ever been in her life. Not only more
terrified. More excited, more wanton... more *lustful*.
Erotic flames had licked their cunning and treacherous

way through every cell of her body, to places she'd never realized existed.

And she had *loved* it.

Panic raced through her veins as she put a hand up to tidy her hair. 'I won't,' she gasped, dragging air into her lungs, 'I won't—it won't be a part of—'

He snatched her hand from her hair, and wove his fingers through hers, roughly. 'You will. And you'll want it. I promise you...you'll want it. On our wedding night, I'll come to you...make no mistake about that. And I'll make love to you as you've never been made love to before.'

He led her to the door of her grandmother's cottage, but before he left he added, with a grim smile that increased her distress a thousandfold, 'Count on that, Greer, if you count on nothing else.'

CHAPTER TEN

GREER told Jem her news the next morning over breakfast. She was surprised that her grandmother seemed so *un*surprised.

'Praise be to heaven.' Jem's lips curved in a smile—no, Greer decided with a trace of amusement, not so much a smile as a smirk, as if her grandmother had not only had prior knowledge of this new development, but had also had a hand in engineering it. Funny old thing...

'I *told* you, didn't I,' Jem went on, 'that the three of you looked like a family! I've always thought you and Colby Daken were meant for each other.'

'But Gran,' Greer protested, 'it won't be a real marriage. I'm only doing it for Jamie—'

'I've seen the way that man looks at you, girl. If this doesn't turn out to be a real marriage, I'll eat my hat—the one I wear when I go to church at Thanksgiving. The yellow straw, with the cartwheel brim, festooned with tasty plastic leaves and masses of delicious vinyl fruit.'

Greer couldn't help laughing. 'Oh, Gran...'

'At any rate,' Jem was suddenly serious, 'if your decision to marry Colby will keep Jamie from your aunt Cecilia's influence, then the pair of you have my blessing. What my son saw in that woman, I'll never know. It was the biggest disappointment of my life, when Taylor told me he'd proposed to her. There was no telling him what she was really like. He couldn't see past her beauty, couldn't see what a superficial creature she was. And then...' She *tut-tutted,* and shook her head.

154

And then history had repeated itself, with Eleanor and Colby. Jem didn't say it, but she didn't need to. Greer could see by the pursing of her grandmother's lips that she and Jem were thinking the same thing:

How could men be so dumb!

Colby turned up with Jamie later on, and after being warmly congratulated by Jem, he said,

'Jamie, tell your aunt Greer what you said to me when I told you of our plans to marry.'

Greer dragged her gaze from Colby—something she found almost impossible to do!—and fixed it on Jamie, telling herself desperately to concentrate on *him*, not his father.

Jamie pushed up his glasses. 'I only said . . .'

His father ruffled his hair. 'Go on.'

Jamie gulped. 'I only said . . . that would be fine with me.'

'That's all?' Colby's tone was teasing.

Jamie grimaced, and shuffled his feet embarrassedly. Then the rest of his words tumbled out in a headlong rush. 'I said it would be fine and could it please be soon.'

'Oh, Jamie.' Greer crossed the room quickly and crouching down, embraced him. 'It *will* be fine, I promise you . . . and it will be as soon as we possibly can arrange it.'

Jamie put his arms around her and hung on grimly. He didn't say another word, but he didn't need to. Greer felt the prick of tears at his intense response, and knew that everything between them was indeed going to be *very* fine.

'Would you like some lemonade, Jamie?' Jem asked.

'Yes, please.' Jamie's voice wavered ever so slightly.

As he slipped away and crossed to the table, Greer straightened . . . and found herself facing Colby. She blinked quickly, only to find him staring at her, as if something about her had taken him unawares. Was it her tears? Had he noticed them . . . and did it bewilder him that she was already so emotionally attached to his son?

She realized they hadn't yet spoken to each other.

'Good morning,' she murmured, wanting to look away but finding it impossible to break eye contact.

'And good morning to you.' He curved a hand around her nape to pull her to him, and Greer yielded helplessly. The pressure of his mouth was light, his lips warm, his taste as fresh and sweet as the morning dew. When he drew back, he let his fingers linger for a moment at her nape, unfurling ribbons of exquisite sensation down her spine.

Greer felt emotion tighten her throat muscles till she thought she might choke. She didn't look at Jem, but knew by her grandmother's smug tone as she offered Colby a cup of coffee that she was sure her promise to eat her fruit-laden hat was one she would *not* have to keep.

Colby excused himself and Jamie after they'd finished their drinks.

'I promised Chris yesterday that the three of us would go for a sail in the *Sprite,* do a bit of fishing.' He glanced at Greer. 'I'd invite you to come along, but since we told the girls it's to be a men-only thing . . .' He shrugged, but there was a twinkle in his eyes.

'That's all right,' Jem said. 'Greer's already promised to drive me to church.'

Which she had.

And by the time they got back, it was close to noon. After Greer parked the car, Jem went inside, and Greer strolled down to the water's edge. She put a hand above her eyes to shade them from the sun as she looked out over the lake. There was no sign of Colby yet, but she guessed he'd be coming back soon.

She turned and went back up to the cottage. Her grandmother had already changed from her elegant linen suit to a loose shirt and baggy shorts. And on the table, steaming and savory, was the chicken casserole Greer had whipped up and popped in the oven before they went out.

'Mmm, smells delicious,' Jem said. 'Thank goodness I feel better today. I could eat the proverbial horse!'

'This is light and nourishing. Much better than any horse!' Greer said as she dished out two generous helpings.

When lunch was over, Greer washed the dishes, and as she stood at the kitchen window, she saw a small boat in the distance; even from far away, she recognized the *Sprite*.

She draped the dish towel over the plastic rack, and turned to her grandmother, who was putting the dishes away.

'Gran, did you really mean it earlier when you said you were feeling much better?'

'I'm right as rain now, dear.'

'Would you mind if I take off for home now? So much has happened this weekend . . . I'd really like to be on my own, to think things over.'

'I don't mind . . . but will Colby?'

Greer shrugged. 'He has my phone number. He can call me if he needs to discuss anything.'

'Will you come back next weekend?'

'I'm . . . not sure. Depends on the progress I've made. There'll be so much to do . . . caterers, church, flowers—'

'You'll wear Lorna's wedding gown?'

'Oh, yes. Mom's headpiece may need modernizing, but that won't be a problem—I can have it done in the workshop. Gina's especially good at that sort of thing—'

'What can I do to help? Oh, if only I had kept on my house in town we could have had such a lovely wedding! My garden was always such a show in July!'

'We'll have a lovely wedding, Gran, wherever it is. And if I can think of any way you can help, I'll phone during the week and let you know.'

'It'll be difficult to get things arranged at such short notice.' Jem made a worried sound.

'Don't fuss, Gran. I've made lots of contacts in my business—I'll pull a few strings, call in a few favors.'

'But Colby said three weeks...it's such a short time!'

'It will be long enough. I promise you.'

It was...but only just, and only with Colby's help.

The following Thursday he turned up at her office, unexpectedly.

'Where's Jamie?' she asked, as she tried to catch her breath. 'Isn't he with you?'

'He's at the cottage...with Alice Kerr.'

'Oh...I didn't realize the nanny would be starting so soon.' Catching her breath wasn't easy. Colby was wearing khaki chinos and a polo shirt in the same dazzling blue as his eyes; just looking at him made her feel as if she was about to hyperventilate.

'She drove up on Monday and has already settled in nicely.'

'Wonderful.' Colby was so close, she wanted to put her arms around him, put her head on his chest. She crossed to Cindy-baby and fidgeted with the cinnamon silk draped over the mannequin's perfect breasts. 'Look, thanks for dropping by, but I have a lot to do...people to phone...I've never arranged a wedding before and I hadn't realized everything would be so solidly booked up already. My church doesn't have a free slot till October, and as for the reception, all the nicest places are—'

'I guessed you might be having a problem...that's why I'm here. This isn't just a social call, Greer.' He tapped her shoulder, making her turn around. 'I've been looking at houses the last couple of days, and I've found one I think is perfect for us. I want you to see it.'

'Can't that wait?' Greer wove a distraught hand through her hair and tried to quell the feeling that everything was falling apart around her. 'I really don't have time to look at houses. Besides, I'm sure that whatever you choose will be fine with me—'

'Greer, don't panic—'

'I'm not!' Her voice shook.

'Yes,' he said softly, 'you are. Look, this won't take long...and I want to move on it as soon as possible. When you see the property, I think you'll understand why.' He crossed to her desk, and scooped up her bag. 'A couple of hours—' his smile was coaxing '—that's all.'

Had she ever been able to resist that smile? Greer gave a defeated sigh, and took her bag. 'All right,' she said. 'As long as it's just a couple of hours.'

The house was situated in Rosedale, one of the loveliest areas in Toronto. The two-story mansion was old and mellow, with walls of faded pink brick, cream-painted trim and a front garden adrift with antique roses, lacecap hydrangea and wisteria. Greer fell in love at first sight.

'You may have heard of Marcia Langdon?' the agent asked as she unlocked the front door.

'The interior designer?' Greer walked into the hall, and found it furnished in a contemporary style that appealed to her immensely. A small frown tucked her brows together. 'This—' she waved a hand around '—looks so familiar.'

'The house was featured in *Best Homes* last month. Perhaps you saw the spread?'

'Yes.' Greer felt Colby's palm in the small of her back and had to resist an almost overwhelming urge to lean

back and put her head on his shoulder. 'Of course, that's
it.'

'Marcia bought this place in the fall,' the agent said,
'and redecorated it with the intention of moving in, but
then decided to sell it. The property has just come on
the market, but there's been a lot of interest in it already.'

The agent showed them over the main floor and the
fully finished basement before taking them upstairs. She
kept the master bedroom till last, and when Colby and
Greer started checking it out, she said, 'I'll wait for you
down in the study—second room on your left along from
the foot of the stairs. Take as long as you need, talk
things over—and don't forget all the furnishings are included, if you want them. When you're ready, I'll show
you over the gardens.'

After she left, there was an awkward silence. Ironic
that she had deposited them in the master bedroom,
Greer mused. Had she sensed the sexual tension vibrating between her two clients? From the corner of her
eye she could see the fabulous canopied bed with its
luxurious duvet and pale satin edged pillows... inviting,
tempting...

Clearing her throat, she crossed to the window. It
looked down, she saw, onto an enormous back garden
with a sparkling blue pool, fruit trees, a velvety green
lawn, crazy-paved paths, a cedar gazebo... and at the
far end a holly hedge, beyond which sloped a deep treed
ravine.

'It's beautiful.' As Greer breathed out the words,
Colby moved into place behind her. He rested his hands
on her hips, the pressure so light it was almost
unnoticeable.

'Over there,' he said, 'by the gazebo and the trellis of
roses, I thought would be an ideal spot for the ceremony.
And over there, on that lawn to the west of the pool,
we can have the reception. We'll have a marquee, of
course with a dance floor...'

For a moment, Greer didn't take in what he was saying. When it clicked, she felt a dizzying sensation in her head.

She turned, and as she did, his hands dropped away. He slipped them into the pockets of his chinos.

'You mean...we'd have the wedding here?' she asked.

'It would be perfect, wouldn't it?'

'Oh.' Dreamily Greer turned and looked out again. It would, indeed, be perfect. But as reality set in, her dreams came tumbling down. It would never be perfect, not when Colby felt about her as he did. Oh, he'd insisted he didn't dislike her, and yes, he was prepared to marry her...but only because he had no other option. It was marry her or risk losing Jamie. Tears misted her eyes; she blinked them away. But before she could turn again, she felt Colby's arms slip around her waist, felt him pull her back against him, the way she'd yearned to be just minutes ago.

'You like it?' His chin rested gently on her head.

Oh, yes, she liked it. Liked to have his arms around her, liked to lean back like this against his chest. 'Yes,' she said, 'I do...like it. But we need it so soon. Have you checked if you can negotiate an early possession date?' She was wearing a thin cotton dress; through it, she could feel the steady beat of his heart against her spine.

'Yes, that's no problem.' His grip around her waist tightened. 'I look forward to gaining early possession.'

Oh, Lord...Greer closed her eyes...early possession. The way he'd said those two words, she'd known he was referring not to the house. Once they were married, he would, indeed, be seeking early possession...and she would have to draw on every bit of steely resolve she could muster, in order to repel his advances. She would have to convince him, once and for all, that she would never let him make love to her. And she would have to tell him that, if he insisted on having his way, it would be rape.

Chilled by the thought, she felt her heart shudder. Inhaling deeply, she grasped his wrists and removed his hands from her waist. She walked a step or two from him.

'It's a lovely house, Colby.' She managed to keep her voice level. 'If this is the one you want, I'm all for it. Shall we go down now and take a walk through the gardens?'

Colby called Greer that evening to say negotiations were complete, and the house would be theirs on Monday.

'It'll be in our joint names,' he said, 'so we'll have to get together at the lawyer's office on Monday morning to sign all the papers. Can you be available?'

'It's not necessary to put my name on the title deed—'

'I want it that way.' His tone brooked no argument. 'Now, let's get together tomorrow to talk about caterers, minister and whatever else we need to talk about. We'll share the load, Greer... because that's the way our marriage is going to be. A partnership in every way.'

After they hung up, though the burden of getting ready for their wedding day had been somewhat lightened, Greer was aware of a heavy feeling in her heart. A partnership. Colby was expecting too much of this marriage; far more than she would be able to give. What would happen when he discovered she wouldn't share his bed? Would he revert to his original plan and take a mistress?

The pain she felt at the prospect was like no pain she'd ever felt before. And as she winced from it, she finally realized the full and awful implications of what she'd done when she'd offered to marry Colby. She had put him in an untenable position. She knew deep in her heart he would never force himself on her; so if he wanted sex—and there was no doubt that he would want sex—

he would have to look for it outside of marriage. And when he did, that would make him an adulterer.

And she knew what he thought of adulterers.

She drew in a shivering breath, and with a sob, buried her face in her hands. What a terrible dilemma she was going to thrust on him. How would he resolve it?

The days leading up to the wedding whipped by for Greer in a blur of frenzied activity. She and Colby pored over recent copies of *Bride's* magazine, and a *Guide to Planning the Wedding Day* she'd picked up at her local library. Then they wrote out lists, and divided out the essential tasks. Some they carried out together, such as finding a band, sending out invitations, deciding on a dinner menu. Others they did separately.

Sometimes Greer became so light-headed as she rushed around that she got the crazy feeling she was watching herself on film...with the film set at Fast Forward. At other times she found herself standing stock-still, her mind utterly blank, as she tried with a feeling of desperation to remember what it was she had just moments ago set out to do.

But in the end, everything got done. Tarling's Tent and Awnings erected a huge marquee two days before the wedding. The catering crew swarmed in and set up tables. A dance floor appeared as if by magic. AAA Pool Maintenance vacuumed the pool. Gardeners weeded the many flower beds, deadheaded the roses and mowed the lawns so closely that when the men left, their large boot prints remained on the grass as if it had been the plushest of emerald carpeting.

After the Friday evening rehearsal dinner, Greer drove directly from the restaurant to her workshop to pick up her heirloom headpiece, which Gina had skilfully modernized. And before she ran back to her car, she took a sheet of paper from her purse and ticked off the last item there, on her list of Things To Do Before The

Wedding Day. Then, with a heartfelt 'Yippee!' of relief, she crumpled the paper into a tight ball and tossed it in the nearby garbage.

At five thirty-five the following afternoon, a long white limousine glided into the driveway of the Rosedale mansion and disgorged its passengers. Greer stood still for a moment, clutching her bouquet of peach roses, while Gillian, her bridesmaid, adjusted the hem of her silk-faced satin-and-organza wedding gown. The weather was perfect, the sky hazy blue, with just one or two drifting clouds, and a breeze so gentle it didn't disturb Greer's hair, which fell in a style of elegant simplicity around her lightly tanned shoulders.

'This dress is absolutely stunning.' Because Gillian was bent over, her voice was muffled by the balloon sleeves of her own dress, an organza gown the same peach-pink as Greer's bouquet. 'I love the way the lace accents at the neckline are repeated at the hem. Your mother had excellent taste.' She straightened. 'Now let me arrange your veil—'

'*I need to pee.*'

With careful fingers Gillian arranged the veil. 'No,' she said, 'you do *not* need to pee. You went to the bathroom before we left. It's just nerves. Now take a deep breath and concentrate on something other than your waterworks.'

The faint strains of organ music drifted through the air from behind the house, and as Greer tilted her head, the sun glanced into the limo's side mirror, and the bright rays bounced from there into her eyes, momentarily blinding her.

But a few minutes later she was dazzled even more, when she walked along the path in the back garden, toward the trellised arbor with its glorious cascade of yellow, peach and cream roses...and caught her first glimpse of Colby.

Dressed in a tux, he looked more handsome than she'd ever seen him, and the unmistakable darkening of his eyes as he watched her approach was clear evidence that he, too, liked what he saw. More than liked...

Her pulses fluttered wildly, she almost missed a step, almost lost time with the music. Get a grip, she told herself, get a grip. Stand well away from him. When she reached Colby, she did just that, but with his eyes now fixed on the minister, he edged closer to her, so that his arm was pressed against her own. She felt her heart tremble.

She loved this man. She always would.

And it was a love that would only grow deeper with time.

Whatever the future held for them, she decided right there and then, she was going to make this day special. She would banish from her mind all the misunderstandings that stood between them. And she would pretend Colby was as deeply in love with her as she was with him.

It would be a fantasy, she acknowledged in a quiet corner of her heart, but she could have nothing more.

'Dearly beloved, we are gathered here today...'

Jem's minister had been coaxed into squeezing the Daken wedding into his busy schedule, but the only slot available on the Saturday they'd chosen was late in the afternoon.

'Five-thirty,' he'd said, with an apologetic smile.

Colby and Greer had told him they were delighted to accept his offer. And they had been.

Now as the Reverend Alan Pederson intoned the opening words of the wedding service, Greer tried to focus on what he was saying, tried not to think of the effect Colby's closeness was having on her. But it was impossible; she could think of nothing else...

And when Colby kissed her after the ceremony was over, she was so shaken by the passion she felt in him that her heart quaked fearfully. A kiss was *never* going to be enough to satisfy this man. Her fantasy wavered... and fell apart. How could she even *begin* to pretend everything was wonderful, when later tonight she and Colby were going to end up engaged in a horrible battle. And whoever 'won' the battle, in the end they would both be losers. The knowledge was like a threatening storm cloud hovering on the horizon.

For the next few hours, Greer pasted a smile on her face, and pretended she *was* having a wonderful time, while all evening the knots in her stomach were clenching tighter and tighter. And after the band started up, she could tell by the increasingly intimate way Colby held her when they danced together that he was impatient to be alone with her.

Just after nine, his impatience gave out.

Someone had dimmed the lights; she and Colby were dancing an old-fashioned waltz together, and by the time the music drifted to a stop, he was holding her so close she could feel every hard contour of his body against her own.

With applause rippling all around them, Colby put his arm tightly around her waist and led her off the floor.

'Let's get out of here.' His voice was taut, his hand moving up and down her back with an urgency that threw her into a panic.

'You want to... leave?'

He ran his hand down her arm, possessively; circled her wrist with one hand. 'It's time.' The husky timbre of his voice made her panic escalate.

'All right.' Cheeks flushed, she glanced around. 'I wonder where Gillian is—she promised to come upstairs with me when I changed, and pack my dress in tissue...'

Colby reached out and touched the delicate guipure lace adorning the portrait neckline of the gown. 'This was your mother's dress?' His fingers lingered, brushed her skin.

Greer felt an odd tingling in her breasts, tried unsuccessfully to ignore it. 'Yes.' Little more than a whisper.

'She would have been proud of you today. You were a very lovely bride.'

All around them, couples were mingling, chatting, laughing. They seemed to Greer to be part of another world. Her own world, at this moment, consisted of only Colby and herself... his fingertips, still lingering on the lace... and on the silken skin at her collarbone.

'Thank you.' Greer's pulses raced off as Colby's hand slid over her shoulder to cup her nape. Fight him, she told herself... but instead she raised her face to his, lost...

'Greer.' Gillian's voice jerked her back to reality. 'Did I hear you say you were ready to leave?'

Colby's hand tightened around Greer's nape for a moment, and then he dropped his arm. 'Yes,' he said. 'We're ready.'

Greer's going-away outfit was an elegant linen suit from Holt Renfrew, the navy V-neck top and straight skirt trimmed with off-white. She had splurged on a pair of Bruno Magli pumps... and also on elegant white gold earrings and a matching bracelet, to coordinate with the wedding ring she and Colby had chosen together at Birks.

Despite her protestations that she didn't want an engagement ring, Colby had insisted, and when she'd stubbornly refused to choose, he'd done the choosing himself and settled on two emeralds in an intricate twist setting. It was an exquisite ring.

Tissue paper rustled, a long zipper rasped closed, a closet door snapped shut. The sounds brought Greer back to the present, to the master bedroom where she'd just changed.

'There.' Gillian looked at Greer with an expression of satisfaction. 'Your mother's dress is preserved for pos-

terity. And now, if you can stop admiring that gorgeous
engagement ring, we can perhaps go and look for your
equally gorgeous new husband!'

'He *is* gorgeous, isn't he.'

'He's one in a million . . . but then, so are you. When
you stood up together, I thought you the most attractive
couple I've ever seen. And it was the *prettiest* wedding.
Can't imagine how you did it, in such a short time. The
dinner was out of this world, and the flower arrangements, too. And didn't your Gran look stunning in that
purple hat? I hope I look half as good when I get to be
her age. Did I tell you I love your house? You were so
lucky the owner wanted to sell it fully furnished!'

'Colby said if I want, I can make changes, but I like
it just the way it is . . .'

Only half listening to Gillian's light chattering, she
walked with her friend from the bedroom and down the
wide steps of the bleached oak circular staircase. But
when they got to the bottom, Lisa came rushing around
the corner. She stopped abruptly at the sight of them.

'Gillian, there you are! Harry's been looking everywhere for you—he was afraid you might have gone.'

'Harry?' Gillian looked puzzled.

'The best man—Colby's old chum—'

'Oh, they told me his name was Henry. He's Harry?'

'His name's Henry but everyone calls him Harry—'

'*Harry's* looking for me?' Gillian's eyes sparkled. 'The
man's a dreamboat! Thanks, Lisa . . .' Her long legs took
her away with quick but elegant strides, and Greer was
left with Lisa.

They both chuckled, and then Lisa said, 'What a
charming outfit, Greer. You and Colby are ready to go?'

'Mmm. I'm just going to look for him. I've been
longer than I meant . . . he's probably outside with Jem.'

They started walking along the corridor, but hadn't
gone far when Lisa stopped and put a hand on
Greer's arm.

'Honey.' Her eyes were serious. 'I'm glad I got this chance to talk with you for a moment. I just want to let you know how happy Brad and I are that you and Colby have finally sorted things out. You did the right thing, letting him know what *really* happened that night eight years ago—'

'Lisa.' Greer's tone was tight. 'Colby still doesn't know the truth.'

For a moment, Lisa's eyes had a blank expression, and then they widened in dismay. 'You mean...you haven't told him? Colby doesn't know that it was *Eleanor* who was making out with Brad that night? He still thinks it wa—'

Lisa's gaze had been caught by something behind her; she stopped in midword, as white as if she'd seen a ghost, a guttural sound coming from her throat. Greer frowned, but even as she started to turn around, Lisa whispered *'Colby!'* and Greer froze, her gaze fixed on Lisa with growing horror.

Lisa had put a hand to her throat. 'Omigosh, Colby, I didn't know you were...'

How long had Colby been there? He must have been in the study; the door was just two feet away. He had been in there, waiting for her. He had chanced to hear...and had discovered...

Greer felt as if an icy hand was on her spine. Pushing her. Forcing her to turn. But she didn't want to turn, didn't want to see. Yet in the end, she had no choice. She knew she had to look at Colby sometime. Heart thudding, pulses juddering, she turned, slowly, and found herself face-to-face with the last person she wanted to be there at that moment. 'Colby...' The word came out on a moan. She slumped sideways against the wall, resting her shoulder against the paneled surface. 'Oh, Colby...'

She wanted to look away, but couldn't. His face was bleached of color, his bones unnaturally sharp under his tautened skin, his eyes as stark and barren as a winter dawn. He wasn't looking at her; he was looking at Lisa.

'Are you saying...' His voice seemed to Greer to be waving up and down, and coming from very far away—which was bewildering since he was standing less than a hand sweep from her. 'Are you saying it was *Eleanor*, not Greer, who was... involved... with your husband?'

Lisa's gaze swiveled to Greer. There was anguish in her expression, but also pleading. Without any words, she was begging Greer to understand what she was going to do. And when Greer saw that look, she flinched as if Lisa had slapped her. *No, Lisa, please...*

Lisa closed her eyes for a moment, then drew in a deep breath, and looked back at Colby.

'Yes,' she said, with a weary gesture, 'Eleanor was the one. She walked along the beach after Brad, she threw herself at him. Greer just happened to be in the vicinity. She'd gone for a walk along the beach because she couldn't sleep....'

Colby brushed his forearm over his eyes, hard, as if he would wipe Lisa from his vision, and wipe from his mind everything she had just said. Then with agonizing slowness, he turned his gaze on Greer. He looked at her as if she was a stranger. A stranger he didn't want to know. 'Why,' he asked, his voice raw with pain, 'didn't you tell me?'

Greer felt as if her throat was closing. 'You never asked.' Tears threatened, and she blinked fiercely to stop them, but her efforts were in vain.

Lisa said, in a low apologetic voice, 'Greer, honey, I'm so sorry. I know you didn't want Colby to find out the truth, you wanted to protect him, but—'

'It's okay, Lisa. Not your fault. None of it.'

Lisa expelled her breath heavily. After a brief hesitation, and a last look at Greer's tear-stained face, she whispered, 'I'll be off then.' She turned and walked away along the lobby. The sound of her unsteady footsteps on the parquet floor died in moments to a faint echo.

Greer felt as if her heart was breaking. But that, she sensed, was nothing compared to how Colby must be feeling. He knew now that Eleanor had betrayed him. She could only guess at his torment. And the last thing he would want at this moment would be to go on a honeymoon.

'Colby.' His name came out waveringly. 'It's all right, we don't have to go through with this...'

He stared at her, as if he wasn't really seeing her, and for the first time she noticed he had changed out of his tux. He was wearing a navy open-neck shirt, and a pair of cotton twill pants. 'What? What did you say?'

'I know how much you loved Eleanor, and I know how you must be feeling. You probably want to be alone—'

'You say you know how I must be feeling?' Colby's lips were white. 'You couldn't be more wrong about that.' He grasped her arm with hard fingers and ushered her forcefully along the lobby, and Greer found she had to run to keep up, because for the very first time she could remember, Colby didn't slow his pace to accommodate her shorter strides.

'Let's get out of here,' he said grimly. 'It's a long drive to the cottage.'

CHAPTER ELEVEN

COLBY switched off the engine of his new Jaguar, slid the keys into his shirt pocket and slumped back in his seat.

As the engine's sound faded, he half turned to look at the figure reclining beside him. He'd adjusted Greer's seat to a more comfortable position a while back, after he'd noticed she was dozing off. She'd protested she wasn't tired, but within minutes she'd dropped off to sleep.

She was still asleep.

A three-quarters full moon slanted through the windscreen. It silvered her pale hair, highlighted her gray eyeshadow, accentuated the sweet curve of her lips. She was, Colby reflected with a dragging ache in his heart, lovelier than an angel. And with her head nestled sideways on the velvet seat, her hands clasped together under one cheek, she looked so peaceful he hated to disturb her.

She looked not only peaceful but innocent. And she *was* innocent. He stifled an anguished groan—a groan laden with remorse and with head-pounding guilt. How could he have been so *stupid?* How could he have been so *blind?* How could he have—

Greer stirred. Blinked. Saw him watching her.

She regarded him for a long moment, her eyes dark, and as unfathomable as the lake at its deepest. Then, in a voice still husky from sleep, she murmured, 'Are we here?'

'Yes.' He switched her seat to the upright position, and the adjustment brought her smoothly to his eye level.

It also brought him a wave of her perfume, and its subtle sensuality threatened his shaky self-control. 'Still tired?'

'I'm fine now.' Greer averted her head, fumbled with her seat belt. 'Was the road busy?'

'No, the traffic was light.'

'What time is it?'

'Just past midnight.'

'Oh, I thought it might be later...'

Small talk, Colby thought—as if they were strangers. Which was what they were to each other, now. Once they had been friends. He had destroyed that friendship.

Beyond repair?

He opened her door for her. She got out. She stood straight, spine erect, slim and elegant... but, he sensed, so tense that if a mouse were to squeak behind her, she would scream. He opened the trunk and extricated her small case and his travel bag.

'You didn't bring much, did you!' He clicked the trunk shut. 'I imagined,' he went on, attempting a teasing tone but failing, 'that you'd pack a trunk of designer clothes.'

'Had we been going to Paris I might have done just that.' A faint smile warmed her voice. They walked along the path to the cottage. 'But since we both wanted to come to the lake, all I've packed are bikinis and shorts.'

'Now that we're here, you're not disappointed, are you?' Colby put the bags down, opened the screen door, kept it open with his hip as he retrieved the cottage keys from his shirt pocket. 'We could have gone anywhere—Paris, New York, San Francisco, Hawaii, the Caribbean...'

'No. This is my favorite place in the world.'

'And we have it all to ourselves.'

'I know Alice and Jamie are spending the week in Toronto with Jem... but the Piersons—'

'They're going on to Florida, after the reception, to visit Brad's grandparents.' Colby pushed the door open, clicked on the entranceway light.

He saw Greer hesitate on the stoop for a second, before she went inside. Had she been waiting for him to carry her over the threshold? She was a romantic; Colby knew that from way back, and he hated to disappoint her...

But that disappointment was going to be only temporary. His heartbeats gave an unsteady lurch as he thought of the surprise he'd prepared for her... the surprise he'd set in motion almost three weeks before, long before he'd learned the truth. He prayed that it would show Greer, in ways no words could, that he had, from the very beginning, wanted this marriage to work.

And he prayed that it would help heal the wounds he'd inflicted...

Because he knew now that he had inflicted wounds. Knew now that he had hurt her unbearably. What he *had* to know was if she could ever forgive him. He had been too shocked, earlier, to put the question.

But he was going to ask it.

And he was going to ask it tonight.

Greer stepped out of the shower in the master bedroom's en suite bathroom, and tossed her plastic shower cap on the counter. She toweled herself dry and slipped on her white lawn nightie, the scalloped hem fluttering to her ankles.

As she brushed her hair, she saw in the mirror that her expression was strained, her eyes darker than the forest outside, her cheeks paler than the moon. Her lips twisted sadly; this was not the kind of image one would expect of a bride on her wedding night. But this was no ordinary wedding night...

For the past three weeks, she'd been tormented by the possibility that she wouldn't find the inner resources to fight off Colby's sexual advances; now there was no longer any need to keep her virginity a secret. But judging by the anguish she'd seen in his eyes when he'd learned Eleanor had been unfaithful, she was sure the last thing on his mind would be making love...to her, or to anyone else. He was distraught; he must also be bitter and disillusioned.

'Greer?' There was a soft tap on the door. 'Are you finished in there?'

She tightened her grip on the handle of the brush. 'Yes, coming.' She put down the brush, flexed her fingers, took in a deep breath...and went out to join her husband.

It hadn't occurred to her to wonder what Colby might be wearing, but it was with faint surprise that she saw he had changed into casual shorts, though his feet, like her own, were bare. He must have showered in the other bathroom, she noticed; his hair was damp, and a few water drops still glistened like clear beads on his shoulders. His eyes were shadowed, revealing nothing of his emotions as he took in the heavy silk sweep of her brushed-out hair, and the soft, finely pleated fabric of her virginal white gown.

'It's a lovely warm night,' he said. 'Would you like to go for a walk? Unwind? Get the kinks out?'

Unhappiness settled on Greer's shoulders as if it were a dark cloak. Colby was aware he'd misjudged her badly, yet he was making no move to apologize. Was he going to act as if the past had never happened? Or was he too upset to talk about it? Either way, this night was going to be a disaster.

Walking together but apart, they crossed the lawn and on down the beach. When they reached the water's edge, Colby said, 'Let's go out onto the jetty.'

The wooden structure dipped and tilted lazily under their feet, and once, when she swayed a little with it, Colby put out a hand and clasped her wrist briefly to steady her.

When they reached the end, Greer rested her elbows on the wooden railing, and looked out over the lake. The moon glinted on the water, and a breeze skimmed the surface, creating snakes of silver that slithered endlessly and with mercurial speed over the inky waves. It was, Greer thought, a sight lovely enough to soothe any soul...yet she knew that more than the beauty of nature was needed to repair her own.

That would need a miracle, and she had lost her faith in miracles.

'Greer...'

She turned. Colby was standing away from her, his hands hanging at his sides. His eyes were fixed on her, and the moonlight reflected in the blue irises, emphasizing their clarity. She leaned back against the railing, and waited.

'We have to talk,' he said, 'about Eleanor.'

At last. Greer felt tension pluck apprehensively at her heart, felt perspiration prick tiny moisture pearls above her upper lip. 'I know,' she said...and wished they were anywhere but here at Lake Trillium, where the poignancy of the soft summer night brought all the old happy memories of Colby and herself to life again. They danced all around her, jeering at her, mocking her with their perfection. Oh, why had he not taken her into the study at the Rosedale house and talked with her there? It would have been so much easier to bear.

She put her hands behind her, curled them tightly around the lower railing...and wished she hadn't. Under her fingertips, she could feel the 'Greer Loves Colby' she had secretly carved there with a penknife when she was fourteen. She drew her hands away and twined them together at her waist.

'Greer—'

'Colby.' Her interruption came in a rush. 'I'm so sorry you had to find out the truth about that night—I never meant you to—Lisa was right when she said I wanted to protect you. And despite what you said earlier, I *do* know how you must be feeling—'

'Because you believe that when Eleanor died, I was still as besotted with her as I was when I married her.'

Colby had spoken so flatly, so matter-of-factly, that for a long moment the implication of his words didn't sink in. Greer stared at him, seeing the breeze catch his hair and sweep it sideways, seeing the moonlight cast a white glow on his hand as he threaded the long strands into place again. She rubbed shaking fingertips over her brow as she grappled to make sense of what he'd said, but why should she feel this confusion? His statement, after all, had been clear, its meaning unmistakable. She swallowed. 'Are you saying you...*weren't?*'

'My marriage to your cousin fell apart more than three years ago, when I found out she'd been involved in a series of affairs—'

Greer made a small sound of protest.

'—that had been going on for some time. How I found out doesn't matter. Let me just say that the feelings I had *then* are the feelings you think I have now. I told Eleanor I was going to divorce her...but she didn't want a divorce—being Mrs. Colby Daken was of the utmost importance to her. It gave her some sort of status in the social circles in which she liked to move. She pleaded with me to give her another chance. But there wasn't a hope in hell of that!'

Greer fought to keep her thoughts from scattering out of her control, but it was hard; her mind was spinning. Colby's marriage to Eleanor had been over? But—

'I moved out right away.' Colby shrugged. 'She collapsed that night, ended up in hospital. I thought it was a ploy to make me change my mind...but it was no ploy. The doctors ran tests and found she was ill. Very ill. They gave her three months.'

Colby's words drowned out every sweet sound whispering through the night air. 'But...she lived...longer...'

'She lived for another two and a half years. The doctors had underestimated the core of strength below her fragile exterior. As I had.' Colby ran a hand over his eyes. 'Of course I'd shelved my plans to start divorce proceedings when I found out she was ill—it would have been monstrous to go on with them. And when Eleanor begged me never to let her mother find out about her affairs, begged me to keep up a pretence of marriage for the little time she believed she had left, I gave in to her request. I had loved her once and I did have compassion for her.

'But I was also consumed with rage—rage at myself, for having been so blind to the kind of woman she was. Thinking about how she'd made a cuckold of me almost drove me crazy so I sought escape in my work. Cecilia was right...I did become a workaholic, but it was the only way I could keep my sanity.

'After her initial hospital stay, Eleanor moved in with Cecilia...which, under the circumstances, was no cause for gossip. She wanted Jamie with her, and knowing he would be losing his mother soon enough, I agreed. A mistake. I discovered, once I got my son back, that not only had Cecilia's coldness crushed all his natural exuberance and spirit of adventure, but Eleanor had turned him against me.'

Greer clutched her arms around herself. 'Oh, Colby, why didn't you tell me all this before?'

'Pride? Male ego?' His laugh was self-derisive. 'I guess I didn't want you to know my marriage had ended up a dismal failure.'

'Your marriage failed.' Greer tried to control the shivering that had beset her. '*You* didn't. The only thing you were guilty of was being dazzled by Eleanor's beauty. I was as gullible as you, where she was concerned...at least, in the beginning. How I used to envy her, in the early years when Jem took me on holidays to Melbourne. I idolized her...it was only when—' Greer broke off. There was no reason why Colby should ever know that Eleanor had set her cap at him after learning how wealthy

Colby's father was. At least she could spare him that. 'She's gone, Colby.' She made a helpless gesture with one hand, as if to say 'What's the point in talking about her now?' She noticed her fingers were shaking, and dropped her hand quickly... but not quickly enough.

Colby frowned. 'You're cold—'

'No, it's not that... it's just... everything's been such a shock—'

'We'll go in.'

Colby took her hand in his, his grip warm, firm, secure. Her heart skipped a beat. What lay ahead now? He still hadn't apologized. Would he ever? Her mind spun with unanswered questions as she and Colby walked back along the jetty, her nightie fluttering around her ankles with each step, her bare feet, and Colby's, making soft padding sounds on the wooden planks.

When they got to the beach, he said, 'Come along to the boathouse for a sec...I have something to show you.'

'You haven't bought another boat, have you? Surely you haven't sold the *Sprite?*'

'No, no new boat.' His grip tightened. 'And I'll never sell the *Sprite.*' The determination of his tone left her in no doubt that he felt the same way about the *Summer Sprite* as she did.

But if not that... then what?

When they reached the boathouse, Greer made to step over to the main door, but Colby stopped her.

'Come around here.'

He led her along the wooden walkway, toward a flight of outside stairs.

'This is new,' she said, surprised.

'It is, and I was relieved that though I managed to sneak up here several times over the last three weeks to supervise the work crew, you were far too busy to come to the lake. Knowing what an enquiring mind you have, I doubt I'd have managed to keep this secret. And it was important that it be kept secret. It's my wedding gift to you.'

'But, Colby, I don't have a gift for—'

He put a finger to her mouth. Shook his head. And stood back, waiting for her to precede him up the stairs.

Biting her lip, Greer started up the narrow flight of steps. When she got to the top, she stopped on the square railed platform to wait for him. Her mind was whirling around. *A wedding gift?* But why on earth would he have stored it up here? The loft was filthy, dusty, cobwebby.

'Colby, our feet are going to get dirty, and—'

'Close your eyes,' he commanded softly.

Greer obeyed, and felt her breath catch as Colby swung her up into his arms. So...*her* feet would stay clean...but what about his? His muscles flexed as he leaned forward, the door latch clicked as he opened it.

The smell of fresh paint was faint but unmistakable. Greer could feel Colby's heartbeat against her shoulder, through the fine lawn of her nightie; could hear the lap of water in the boathouse below, the *slip-slap* of wavelets licking against the stern of the *Summer Sprite*.

'All right.' Colby's voice was husky. 'You may look now.' He slid her to her feet.

As Greer's eyes adjusted to the sudden change from dark to bright, for a moment she saw only the moonlight that streamed through the window overlooking the lake. And then, as the scene before her began to take shape, shock exploded through her with such force she felt her body rock from it. Disbelief...changing swiftly to joy...coursed through her in dizzying waves. Colby had remembered how romantic she was, had remembered her girlhood dreams: he had made those dreams come true...and he had even carried her over the threshold.

'Oh, Colby—' her voice shook '—you remembered.'

'Is it...as you imagined it could be?'

No longer was the loft dusty and bare. The walls and ceiling were glossy white; the window was polished so the panes shone as clear as crystal; the floor had been laid with oak parquet tiles, its hard surface softened by a hooked rug in nautical red, white and blue. And the antique iron bed was queen-size, its luxurious duvet covered in white eyelet cotton with plump matching pillows, the bed itself facing the picture window, just as it had in her girlhood dreams...

So lovers could look out over the lake, and up to the stars.

'It's perfect,' Greer at last managed to whisper.

She moved across the room, to a door that lay ajar. Her throat tightened even further, when she saw, clearly in the moonlight, the trillium-patterned porcelain of a dainty bathroom suite. She turned, and found Colby behind her.

'It's for you, Greer...a place of your own. A place where you can be alone. The cottage is going to be pretty crowded, now that we have Alice...but we'll build on an extra couple of rooms, and I intend to winterize the place. It'll all take a while, though, so meantime...'

Out of everything Colby was saying, Greer retained only one word.

Alone.

He meant this to be a place for her to come *alone*.

Her heart gave a teary wobble, and then plunged with an aching, unbearable disappointment.

She turned from him and walked to the window. Pressing her hands together, she took in a tremulous breath and stared out over the lake.

'Greer, what is it...?'

Colby had come up behind her.

'I hadn't realized,' she whispered, 'that you mean it to be for me...alone... I thought—'

He grasped her shoulders from behind, and turned her around, taking her hands in his. 'Thought what?'

All her love for him, all her despair, welled to the surface, and she couldn't hold back the words she wanted to say.

'I thought—' she stumbled and then went on miserably '—I thought, when I saw what you'd done, that you'd meant this place to be for... us. Oh, I know I told you the night you accepted my proposal that our marriage would be in name only, and I meant that truly when I said it. But things are different now—I no longer have to keep any... secrets... from you.'

I don't have to keep my virginity a secret from you. She didn't say that, because she knew she didn't have to spell it out; Colby would know what she was referring to. 'But you told me you'd... come to me on our wedding night. And when we were dancing, the way you held me, the way you looked at me... I thought... you wanted me. I thought you wanted us to be... together.'

Colby's fingers tightened around hers, so hard she almost winced. Moonlight shone starkly on his face, revealing the agony in his eyes. 'Is that what *you* want? For us to... be together?'

Greer felt tears well up, felt them clog her throat so she could scarcely get out the words she so desperately wanted to say. 'It's *all* I've ever wanted.'

'Are you saying that... you love me?'

'I've loved you almost forever.'

'And are you saying—' his voice shook '—that you've forgiven me?'

Greer's tears ran down her face, till she tasted the salt on her lips. 'Forgiving you,' she whispered, 'is the easiest thing I've ever done.'

'Oh, God...' Colby drew her into his arms, and buried his face against her neck, his lips trembling on her skin. His cheek was pressed to her jawbone, and she felt the unmistakable moisture of his tears. His anguish intensified the pain in her throat till she could hardly bear it. And his arms were so tight around her she could scarcely breathe. 'Of course I wanted us to be together . . . and of course I meant this room to be for us. But tonight, when Lisa spilled out the truth and I realized how I'd misjudged you, I swore I'd give you what you told me you wanted . . . a marriage in name only. I don't deserve you, Greer . . . I don't deserve your forgiveness—how can you forget how I treated you—'

'It's past, Colby—'

He raised his head, framed her face in his hands, his eyes glistening. 'I *knew* I'd lost something precious when our friendship was shattered, but I also felt there was something more . . . a greater loss. I could never figure out what it was. And I couldn't understand why the thought of your being with another man had driven me into such a fury.'

He wove his hands through her hair, and the strands fell through his fingers as if they were rich silk. 'When Eleanor and I came to the lake that summer, I was a man in love with his wife to the point of obsession. And yet, when you raced up the beach to hug me—so beautiful in your innocence—I felt a painful aching in my heart . . . an aching that had no logical explanation. All I knew at that moment was . . . I never wanted you to change. What I understand now is that what I was feeling for you was love . . . the best kind of love, the kind that starts off with friendship, and liking . . . and somehow in the end, miraculously, becomes so much more. I wish I could pinpoint the moment this summer when I fell in love with you, my darling, but I can't. All I know is—I *am* in love with you, deeply in love, and it's a love beyond compare.'

Joy made Greer feel as if she was floating, higher and higher, till she could have touched a star. 'Is this heaven, Colby?' she whispered.

His smile would have lit up the night, had there been no moon. 'Yes, my angel, this is heaven. Our heaven.'

Greer's eyes shone with tears...and with the love she'd been forced for years to keep buried deep in her heart. 'I've waited so long for you to grow up, Colby Daken!'

His laugh was warm, so warm it made Greer's heart glow. At last, at last...

'Didn't you ever get tired of waiting?' He fiddled with the pearl button at the high neck of her nightie, but his gaze was fixed on her eyes.

'Mmm-mmm.' She shook her head. 'Never.'

He raised his dark brows teasingly. 'What about Nick Westmore and Jared Whatsisname...and all those Friday night lovers your grandmother got so riled up about?'

'Friends, Colby. Just friends. All of them.'

'My fist *itched* to grind your surgeon buddy into a pulp when he kissed you that night! I *wanted* you, dammit...and I sure as hell wasn't going to let anybody else have you!'

'So *that's* what made you change your mind about accepting my proposal!' Greer's pulse raced faster as Colby began undoing the buttons of her nightie. 'You were just as jealous of him as I was of Bettina—'

'Ah, so I was right—you *were* miffed when she—'

'*Miffed?* Good Lord, I wanted to claw those huge brown bedroom eyes out by the roots!'

'Which,' Colby said smugly, 'was exactly the effect I was aiming for!'

'Oh, Colby.' Greer smiled happily as she slipped her arms around his waist. 'There's never been anyone else for me but you. My summer love...'

'Your forever love.' His eyes had become hazy with longing, clouded with desire. Her heartbeats flew away beyond her control, as he swept her up in his arms and carried her across to the bed.

'If I'd known we were going to be together tonight,' she whispered, 'I'd have worn black silk...'

His gaze burned into her. 'Any woman can wear black silk,' he murmured. 'You said earlier you didn't have a gift for me?' He lowered her gently onto the bed, and sank down alongside her. 'Don't you realize that your innocence is the most precious gift of all?'

Her nightie had slipped down over her shoulder. Colby caressed the scented skin at her throat, his touch tender, yet possessive. 'Do you remember,' he said softly, 'my telling you that when I made love to you I wanted your hair to be spread out on a pillow, silvered by moonlight?'

'I remember.'

His gaze moved to her hair, as he spread out the silken strands, fanning them over the fine cotton. 'Beautiful,' he said huskily, 'even more beautiful than I'd imagined.'

'You did imagine this, then?'

He trailed a dance of kisses along the shining strands. 'Since we met again ... many, many times ...'

'What else did you imagine?' Greer's voice was shy, yet had a teasing, seductive lilt.

'I imagined this.' Colby brushed a kiss over her brow. 'And I imagined this.' He brushed another over the tip of her nose. 'And I imagined this ...'

His lips claimed hers in a kiss that was better than any *she* had ever imagined. With an ecstatic sigh Greer put her arms around Colby's neck, and surrendered to the urgent power of his body, as with tender love and exquisite skill he took her flying with him to a sensual paradise where the past, and old summer secrets, were forgotten.

But later, as pink ribbons of dawn began to streak the sky and Greer was falling asleep in Colby's arms, she remembered something.

'Colby?' she whispered. 'Are you awake?'

'No,' he said sleepily, 'I'm not.'

She poked him. 'What about Aunt Cecilia? Is your lawyer confident everything's going to be all right now?'

With a drowsy mutter, Colby propped himself up on one elbow. Though his lashes were half closed so that they almost hid the expression in his eyes, she could see the embers of passion still glowing there. But besides the passion, she saw something else. A hint of... sheepishness?

'Colby... what is it?'

'Cecilia has...er...dropped her case. Apparently her decision to sue for custody was a knee-jerk reaction to the news that I'd be settling here. Once she had time to mull the matter over, she realized the very last thing she wanted was to be permanently saddled with a child.'

Greer blinked. 'Whenever did you find out?'

Colby lifted one wide shoulder in a shrug. His eyes didn't quite meet hers. 'The day before the wedding.'

'The day before the wedding?' Greer felt her mind reel. 'But why didn't you tell me?' Suddenly she was wide-awake. More wide-awake than she'd ever felt in her twenty-five years. She sat bolt upright and stared at Colby. 'You didn't need to take a wife after all! You could have called off the wedding! Did you think it was too *late?*'

'It's never too late to call off a wedding.'

'Then why...?'

'Because, my darling, you told me when you proposed that I was the last man on earth you'd choose to marry, and there was always the chance that if you knew Cecilia was out of the picture, you'd opt out of our arrangement.' Colby was looking at her now, his expression so serious Greer felt a funny little shiver run down her spine. 'It was a risk I was not prepared to take. Besides—' his eyes held the suspicion of a twinkle '—I'd promised you I'd have you in my bed by summer's end, and I am a man of my word.'

Oh, dear Lord. Greer's gaze drifted over Colby's beloved features, and she wondered anew at the miracle that had brought him to her. 'You *tricked* me,' she said, trying to scold, but unable to hide the delight she felt at his confession. 'And for that, Colby Daken, you owe me one.'

Colby's mouth slanted in a sensual smile that set Greer's heart racing with delicious anticipation. He slid them both down onto the pillows again and pulled her close. 'Indeed I do,' he murmured. 'And am I to assume, from the provocative way you're arching against me, that you're not interested in accepting credit?'

'My terms,' Greer answered dreamily, 'are strictly "Pay as you go".'

'I *like* your terms. I like them very much.' Colby claimed Greer's lips in a kiss that tingled to the very tips of her peach-frosted toenails. 'After all,' he chuckled, 'building up debts is no way to start a marriage.'

Harlequin Romance®

Delightful

Affectionate

Romantic

Emotional

Tender

Original

Daring

Riveting

Enchanting

Adventurous

Moving

Harlequin Romance—the
series that has it all!

HROM-G

HARLEQUIN PRESENTS®

HARLEQUIN PRESENTS
men you won't be able to resist
falling in love with...

HARLEQUIN PRESENTS
women who have feelings
just like your own...

HARLEQUIN PRESENTS
powerful passion in
exotic international settings...

HARLEQUIN PRESENTS
intense, dramatic stories that will keep you
turning to the very last page...

HARLEQUIN PRESENTS
The world's bestselling romance series!

PRES-G

Harlequin® Historical

From rugged lawmen and
valiant knights to defiant heiresses
and spirited frontierswomen,
Harlequin Historicals will
capture your imagination with
their dramatic scope, passion
and adventure.

Harlequin Historicals...
they're too good to miss!

HHGENR

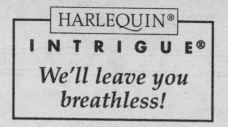

HARLEQUIN®

I N T R I G U E®

We'll leave you breathless!

If you've been looking for thrilling tales of
contemporary passion and sensuous love stories
with taut, edge-of-the-seat suspense—
then you'll *love* **Harlequin Intrigue!**

Every month, you'll meet four new heroes
who are guaranteed to make your spine tingle
and your pulse pound. With them you'll enter
into the exciting world of Harlequin Intrigue—
where your life is on the line
and so is your heart!

THAT'S INTRIGUE—DYNAMIC ROMANCE AT ITS BEST!

HARLEQUIN®

I N T R I G U E®

INT-GENR

LOOK FOR OUR FOUR FABULOUS MEN!

Each month some of today's bestselling authors bring
four new fabulous men to Harlequin American Romance.
Whether they're rebel ranchers, millionaire power brokers
or sexy single dads, they're all gallant princes—and
they're all ready to sweep you into lighthearted fantasies
and contemporary fairy tales where anything is possible
and where all your dreams come true!

You don't even have to make a wish...
Harlequin American Romance will grant your every desire!

Look for Harlequin American Romance
wherever Harlequin books are sold!

HAR-GEN